Bolan raised his glass and drank deeply

"I'm looking for Tony Cipirello," he finally said.

The bartender shrugged, as if the name meant nothing to him, but the Executioner saw his gaze shift to a booth opposite to the bar.

Bolan could see the men seated there reflected in a mirror. One looked like the enforcer Russ Caldwell had described.

The warrior shoved two dollar bills across the counter, then turned and walked to the booth.

"Cipirello," he said coldly.

Antonin Cipirello took his measure for a moment, then asked, "Who the hell are you?"

"It doesn't matter. You leaned on a friend of mine, and I don't like it."

"Who gives a damn what you like?" The enforcer sneered, then reached into his jacket and withdrew a revolver.

The Beretta coughed twice, and Tony Cipirello slumped back in his seat.

Bolan's eyes bored through the remaining mobsters. "Give my regards to Cesare Frenchi." He walked out of the bar and was on the street before anyone but the two terrified men in the booth realized Cipirello had been hit.

MACK BOLAN.

The Executioner

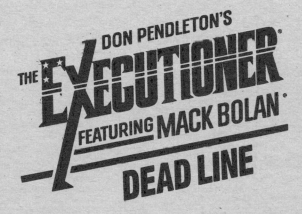

DON PENDLETON'S
THE EXECUTIONER®
FEATURING MACK BOLAN®

DEAD LINE

A GOLD EAGLE BOOK FROM
WORLDWIDE®
TORONTO • NEW YORK • LONDON • PARIS
AMSTERDAM • STOCKHOLM • HAMBURG
ATHENS • MILAN • TOKYO • SYDNEY

First edition October 1989

ISBN 0-373-61130-7

Special thanks and acknowledgment to
Carl Furst for his contribution to this work.

If you kick a man he kicks you back . . . Therefore never be too eager to engage in combat.

Bertolt Drecht, 1928

La Cosa Nostra has rattled this soldier's cage more times than enough. Cut off its head, and it grows another. Bury it in a hole, and it crawls out somewhere else. You can win battles, but you can't quite kill it. But I'll keep coming back until the creature is finally laid to rest. Count on it.

—Mack Bolan

THE
MACK BOLAN®
LEGEND

Nothing less than a war could have fashioned the destiny of the man called Mack Bolan. Bolan earned the Executioner title in the jungle hell of Vietnam.

But this soldier also wore another name—Sergeant Mercy. He was so tagged because of the compassion he showed to wounded comrades-in-arms and Vietnamese civilians.

Mack Bolan's second tour of duty ended prematurely when he was given emergency leave to return home and bury his family, victims of the Mob. Then he declared a one-man war against the Mafia.

He confronted the Families head-on from coast to coast, and soon a hope of victory began to appear. But Bolan had broken society's every rule. That same society started gunning for this elusive warrior—to no avail.

So Bolan was offered amnesty to work within the system against terrorism. This time, as an employee of Uncle Sam, Bolan became Colonel John Phoenix. With a command center at Stony Man Farm in Virginia, he and his new allies—Able Team and Phoenix Force—waged relentless war on a new adversary: the KGB.

But when his one true love, April Rose, died at the hands of the Soviet terror machine, Bolan severed all ties with Establishment authority.

Now, after a lengthy lone-wolf struggle and much soul-searching, the Executioner has agreed to enter an ''arm's-length'' alliance with his government once more, reserving the right to pursue personal missions in his Everlasting War.

1

"Striker, I appreciate your dropping everything to come to Wonderland." Hal Brognola restlessly paced the office, vigorously chewing his unlit cigar.

Mack Bolan had never heard his friend sound more weary. Some of that weariness had been transmitted over the telephone line hours earlier when Brognola had made the call that prompted the Executioner to grab the first flight out of Miami. The two men had worked together for many years—during good times and bad—and they had developed a warm friendship.

"What's the problem, Hal?"

"An operation in Boston turned sour, and I've got to fly up there this afternoon. A damn good agent was murdered this morning. Somebody penetrated his cover. I..." Brognola shook his head. "A good man."

"How can I help?"

Brognola shrugged. "It's your old stomping ground. In fact, some of the people you used to stomp—the Mob."

"New England?" Bolan asked.

"Yeah. You had a kick at the can once, but bad news like that always comes back. A new generation and new rackets, but the same old story. Our guy was working undercover, setting up a case against two of their biggest boys. Now..." The big Fed sighed. "A man is dead, and probably the case died with him. I need you, Striker. Come out to Andrews with me and fly up to Boston. I can use moral support.''

THIRTY MINUTES LATER the two men were aboard a Justice Department Lear jet, waiting for a slot on a runway at Andrews Air Force Base. When the jet was cleared for takeoff, it swung onto the runway and screamed down the tarmac, sweeping away to the east at a steep angle.

"Striker," Brognola began, "everyone knows that air cargo is ripped off at most of the big airports all the time. If a thousand electronic typewriters are shipped, you figure nine-fifty are going to arrive. The shippers accept that. They figure it's just a cost of doing business.''

"They'd rather accept the loss than have to fight the unions," Bolan stated. "It used to be that way on the waterfront, too.''

"Well, it's worse at some of the airports than it ever was on the waterfront. And the losses are getting bigger. Millions of dollars are being lost. They steal everything.''

"A Mafia deal, you think?''

Brognola nodded. "Not all the boys went out to Vegas or muscled in on legitimate businesses like banking and real estate. They're still into all the old reliable stuff—hijacking, loan-sharking, gambling, extortion—''

"And narcotics," Bolan interjected.

"And narcotics," the big Fed agreed. "There's a connection. Suppose the box that contains the electronic typewriter also contains a bag or two of heroin or cocaine? The wise guy who rips off the typewriter also gets the white stuff. It's a way to move narcotics up from Florida, in from the Coast—or wherever.''

"Some combination.''

"When the Mafia controls an air-cargo terminal,'' Brognola continued, jabbing his knee with one finger, "they can move everything through it—hell, sometimes it's even *people*. Both dead and alive. The profits are immense. Start with the cargo they rip off. Hundreds of millions of dollars a year. And who can even guess what they make on the narcotics? They don't own the stuff. They just move it for the owners and make a percentage for their services. Same way with some other things they move."

"The New England Families aren't the only ones involved," Bolan guessed.

Brognola shook his head. "They work Boston Logan chiefly, because it's an international airport with lots of overseas flights in and out. But they're working Providence, Hartford, Bridgeport. Oddly enough, the New York Families have let them have part of the action at Kennedy and La Guardia. I don't have a clue why."

"What about Miami?"

"Absolutely, Miami. Though it's a little harder for them there. We've had a federal task force specially assigned to Miami for years. But...Houston, Dallas, St. Louis—there's some coordination. Has to be. Obviously you can't move something from Boston to Dallas without some coordination between the Families on both ends."

"Overseas flights?"

"Their favorites. So much good merchandise comes in from Europe and Asia. Other places, too. They ripped off part of a load of African primitive sculptures a couple of weeks ago. These guys will steal anything."

"Must have a hell of a fencing operation," Bolan observed.

Brognola nodded. "That's what I'm telling you. They're organized, coordinated. The money is *big*."

"Your money and mine."

"Exactly. The shippers figure the rip-offs are a cost of doing business and just raise prices to cover the losses.

When you buy one of those electronic typewriters, you're paying a few extra dollars for the ones lost in shipping."

"And they've killed a federal agent," Bolan added.

"He's the second. They've also murdered state and local investigators, plus private security guards. These guys are willing to kill to protect their business. And of course, they use their money to buy off cops, district attorneys, even judges. That is, they use money as a last resort. What they'd rather do is scare off investigations—intimidate."

"I've got to admit, Hal, I wasn't aware of the extent of this problem."

"You've had your hands full lately. I've asked you to help out with several missions that have taken your attention away from the home front. You've been out of touch with what the old Families are up to. But you, better than anybody, know how big-time organized crime is."

"Yeah," Bolan replied. "Cut off a head, and it grows another. Bury it in a hole, and it crawls out somewhere else. You can win battles, you can defeat it, but you can't quite kill it."

Brognola frowned. "It's really starting to look that way."

THE JET DESCENDED through dense cloud cover, breaking free of the gloom only a mile and a half from the touchdown point on 33 Left at Logan International.

A federal car—black Ford—rolled out onto the tarmac to meet the Lear as it came to a stop.

"I'm going to introduce you as Major Morrison," Brognola said as they stepped to the door of the Lear. "No point in letting these fellows know they're meeting the Executioner."

"Good enough."

"Not that I don't trust them," Brognola added quickly.

"But no point in opening old wounds," Bolan commented dryly.

The two men waiting in the car were FBI agents—Jack Lindsay and Robert DiRosario. Lindsay had the look of a junior accountant while DiRosario was smoother, more handsome. Both wore rain spotted suits.

Lindsay hurried out of the vehicle to open the rear doors for Brognola and his companion.

"Gentlemen," Brognola announced when they were seated in the car and the doors were closed again, "let me introduce an old friend of mine—Major MacKenzie Morrison. The major happened to be visiting me when your call came, and I asked him to come to Boston with me rather than interrupt our visit. Feel free to talk in front of him. Major Morrison is retired, but had high-level clearance during his career and knows just about everything that's going on. I briefed him on the way up."

The two agents reached over the back of the front seat to shake Bolan's hand, but the warrior judged that neither man accepted the big Fed's story. They were too circumspect to express doubt yet too little skilled at dissimulation to conceal it.

"Do you want to see where it happened?" asked DiRosario, who was driving. "A witness or two might still be around."

"Why not?" Brognola replied.

As DiRosario drove with caution across the busy ramps and roads of the airport, Lindsay turned and began to talk about the murder.

"We wouldn't have heard about the killing for a long time if we hadn't gotten an anonymous tip," he said. "The airport police didn't know Ron was a federal agent. They pegged the murder as a Mob hit, but they had no idea *who*'d been hit. By the time we got here, city and state detectives were on the scene, but they didn't know, either. In fact, they wanted to know what the FBI was doing sticking its nose into the case."

"They'd have found out who he was, in time," Brognola said.

"Sure. Or I suppose they would. But it would have been a day or so, probably. Anyway—"

"Anyway, you got an anonymous tip," Brognola interrupted impatiently. "When?"

"About nine-thirty this morning," DiRosario replied, keeping his eyes straight ahead. "It was a phone call."

"What did the informant say?" Bolan asked. "Did you record it?"

"No, we didn't. We had no reason to know what was coming, and the call was over in ten seconds. What he said was—"

"The caller was a man?"

"Absolutely," Lindsay replied. "He said, 'You'll find a dead Fed out at Logan. Dundee hangar. Pays to be careful, don't it?' Then he hung up."

"A threat?" Bolan asked.

DiRosario glanced over his shoulder, apparently surprised to hear Brognola's friend and guest asking questions as if he, too, were a federal investigator. At that moment it occurred to him that "Major Morrison" might well be just that.

"You could take it for a threat, couldn't you?" DiRosario said. "But it'd have to be some kind of cool guy to call the FBI and make a threat, wouldn't you say?"

"Or some kind of fool," Brognola countered.

"Just one of the boys," Bolan said. "What's Dundee hangar?"

"Dundee Aviation, Incorporated," Lindsay told him. "They operate a small fleet of older planes, all cargo, that aren't licensed for passengers. But they've also got one of the better air-freight facilities at the airport. Good loading and unloading equipment, and a good warehouse that used to be a hangar. They've got good relations with trucking companies, and they freight in from planes and out on trucks, all very efficiently."

"Connected?" Bolan asked.

Lindsay shook his head. "No. Dundee was a World War II pilot, flew C-47s over the Hump, came back here and started the business in 1947. His sons are clean, too. But stuff disappears from their hangar regularly, and they're afraid to try to do anything about it."

"They've got reason to be afraid," DiRosario added. "When Terry Kilbane, who runs Shamrock Air Cargo, tried to roust the wise guys out of his hangar, one of his kids was hit by a car on the way home from school. It was no accident. A ten-year-old girl with multiple fractures of both legs. She still wears a brace."

"Nice guys," Brognola muttered.

"Real sweethearts," DiRosario rasped.

The Dundee hangar-warehouse loomed ahead, and DiRosario pulled to a stop near a small side door that led to the office. They were met just inside the threshold by a heavyset, gray-haired man in corduroy slacks and a plaid shirt. Lindsay performed the introductions.

"This is Mr. Tom Dundee, the president of the company. Tom, this is Hal Brognola, Department of Justice, and Major MacKenzie Morrison."

Dundee shook hands with Bolan and Brognola. "Justice Department," he repeated. "These guys work for you?"

"No," Brognola replied. "We cooperate."

"But the man who was killed did work for you," Dundee said.

"Yes."

"I'm damn sorry about that, Mr. Brognola. I didn't get to know the guy, but I'm sorry he was murdered. But look, you should have told me who he was. You guys should have told me you had an undercover man working in my business. You tell me now that Dundee isn't suspected of anything illegal, but you put an undercover man in my warehouse and didn't tell me. I don't understand that."

"What would you have done if you'd known?" Brognola asked.

Dundee shook his head. "I don't know. What could I have done? I guess I couldn't have prevented what happened."

"You know who did it, don't you?"

"Sure. I mean, I don't know who the triggerman was. I don't have a name I could give you, but I know who's responsible. And so do you. That's something else. Why put an undercover man here to find out what we all know perfectly well?"

"To build a case," Brognola explained. "We can't do anything about what we *know*. We have to have evidence."

"Please don't do me any favors," Dundee said wryly.

"Meaning . . . ?"

"You guys are going to try to stop what's going on? Well, good luck, but don't make me the test case. I don't need broken legs."

"You're scared."

"Major—what is it, Morrison? Yeah, I'm scared. You're damn right I'm scared. There is one favor you can do for me. When you issue a statement, say you never told me you had an undercover agent working here. If certain people thought I did know . . ." His meaning was clear.

Brognola turned to Lindsay. "Do what he asks. We've got to release a statement. Be sure it says that Mr. Dundee didn't know Ron Elliott was a federal agent."

"Ron Elliott, formerly of Army Intelligence?" Bolan asked.

Brognola nodded, startled. "Yeah. You've got a file picture of him there, haven't you, Lindsay?"

The agent opened his briefcase, took out a folder and handed it to Brognola. The big Fed showed the picture to the Executioner.

"You knew Ron Elliott," Brognola said quietly.

"From the old days," Bolan replied gruffly. "From Nam. You say he was a good man. I'm not sure you know how good. I didn't know he worked for Justice."

Bolan glanced at the men who were listening—Lindsay, DiRosario, Dundee—all of them curious, and decided he had said enough. He and Hal Brognola could communicate without words and had been able to for years; Brognola knew the meaning of his glance and the silence into which he then lapsed.

"Okay. Show us where Ron was killed."

Dundee led them into the huge interior of the building that had once been capable of housing two DC-6s, or perhaps three or four DC-3s that were undergoing maintenance. Now it was stacked high with crates and steel shipping containers, and was equipped with forklift trucks and pallets.

The chalked outline of a body showed where Ron Elliott had been found on the floor. His blood still stained the concrete.

"I hate to tell you this, Major, since he was your friend," DiRosario said, "but he was shot once in each knee, then in the head. A message, you know."

Bolan nodded grimly. "Yeah, I know." He faced Brognola. "Has his wife been notified?"

"I called her before you came to my office in Washington."

Bolan turned from the chalked outline on the floor, shaking his head. He couldn't walk away from this one. It was time the "new generation" faced the blazing justice of the Executioner.

2

Mack Bolan walked into a small bar called Popeye's in the shadow of Fenway Park. In an hour the place would be crowded, but right now the game was only in the fifth inning, and the Red Sox fans were still drinking beer in Fenway. Only a few customers with shots and beer chasers sat at the bar, ignoring the prime-time soap on the big color television high on the wall at the end of the room.

Bolan had done what he could to look casual. He was dressed in tan slacks and a khaki nylon jacket over a dark blue shirt. He didn't want to be conspicuous, yet knew he would be. Popeye's was a bar for regulars, and a stranger would stand out.

He scanned the place, saw the man he was looking for—recognizing him from a photograph Brognola had supplied—and took the second stool away from him, ordering a beer. The man glanced at him, then returned his eyes to his shot glass and beer mug.

"Uh, you're Terry Kilbane, aren't you?" Bolan asked, as if he didn't know.

The man looked up, not hostile but not friendly, either—perhaps a little suspicious. He fixed his eyes on Bolan for a moment, then shrugged, nodded and looked down again.

"How's the girl?" Bolan asked.

"What girl?"

"Your daughter. The little girl who got hit by a car."

Kilbane's head snapped around, the hostility that had been missing now etched into his face, hot and angry. He was a big man, a rusty-haired Boston Irishman who probably weighed two-twenty. His big muscles bunched under an open-collared white shirt, and he had big, hammy fists. As he glared at Bolan, the wind visibly went out of him.

Bolan could read the guy. Kilbane thought he was getting another warning and his impulse was to attack. Then he remembered they hadn't come after him, but after his little girl. They could be doing something along the same lines again. He deflated.

"Look, Kilbane, it's not what you think. There are a few people who are concerned about what's going down, people who can do something about it. I need your help."

Kilbane frowned hard. His lips separated as if to say something, but he only frowned and regarded Bolan with silent apprehension. Finally he said, "How do I know I can trust you?"

"From what I know of the situation, you don't have much choice. I need a quick answer to one question—who did it?"

Kilbane drew a deep breath. "You goin' after them? Uh-uh. They'll come after me again in their own special way."

"They won't tie it to you," Bolan assured him. "The guy who ran down your little girl—do you think she's the only person he ever hurt? Guys like that have hundreds of enemies, and how about the man who hired him? How many do you suppose he has?"

"They killed a federal agent the day before yesterday," Kilbane muttered.

"I know all about that. A friend of mine. Same guys?"

"They're all the same guys, friend. A goddamn army of them. You think the punk who wasted the Fed is the same guy who ran down Becky?'' He shook his head. ''Could be, but not likely.''

''The man who sent the guy who ran down Becky,'' Bolan pressed. ''Who is he?''

Kilbane hesitated again, looking around the room as if afraid someone was watching, listening. The other regulars in Popeye's were slumped over their beers or arguing with one another—no one was paying attention to Kilbane and Bolan.

''It's a long story.''

''I know all about it. I know they rip off your air cargo.''

Kilbane sighed and nodded. ''Stuff disappears. It's some of the guys who work for me. They just take it, you know? I can't fire them. That's what I tried to do, and—''

''Union?''

''Well,...they're members, but... Well, I don't say the union is corrupt. The way I figure, the union is forced to accept wise guys as members, the same way I'm forced to hire them and let them steal. You know the worst thing? The shippers and the insurance companies don't complain. Some people are paid off, more people are intimidated. And some guys are getting as rich as hell.''

''A name,'' Bolan repeated firmly.

''Cesare Frenchi,'' Kilbane murmured.

''I've heard the name,'' Bolan said.

Kilbane glanced around again. ''Well, the Frenchi Family has the action at Logan International, as well as some at the New York airports, I hear. Plus all the usual stuff those scum have.''

''And Frenchi sent the hit man to hurt your daughter. You're sure?''

Kilbane shrugged. ''Maybe it was an accident. But if it was, why were a dozen red roses delivered to her hospital room, compliments of Caesar Cartage? That's the Frenchi trucking company. They haul trash from downtown hotels and restaurants, and air cargo from the warehouses at the airport. The flowers were a message, pure and simple."

"Okay, Kilbane," Bolan said. "You never saw me, I never saw you. I'll take care of things from here."

Kilbane nodded. "Yeah. Look, I, uh, I wish I could help you. I really do. But I got too much to lose. You understand, don't you?"

Bolan took a last swallow of beer. "Don't try to help. It's not your line of work. It's mine."

WHEN BOLAN HIT THE STREET outside Popeye's, he had no trouble hailing a rattling, battered cab.

"Where to?" the cabbie asked.

"Where can I find a little action?" Bolan asked.

"Uh, like what kinda action?"

"Well, maybe a chick. Maybe a little angel dust to make it feel better."

The cabbie shook his head. "Maybe you're a cop, maybe a narc. Look, I don't know where you get that stuff. I can take you to a neighborhood where they say it's found, but all I know is what I read in the papers."

"Good enough."

The warrior was a little surprised at where the driver took him—to Cambridge, in the vicinity of Harvard University. The cabbie stopped on a street a little north and east of the university.

"Keep your eyes open," the man advised. "For more reasons than one."

Bolan understood what he meant. Like neighborhoods of its kind everywhere, this one was filled with illicit promise but also with menace. It was a run-down area where respectable people had once lived in respectable houses. Now some of the lots were vacant, choked with weeds and litter, and the buildings dilapidated or vandalized. Businesses had been established on what had been residential streets—a repair garage with half a dozen ramshackle cars parked on the sidewalk as well as the street, a pizza parlor, bars ...

Four loitering blacks sized him up as he walked past them—their gazes narrowed, their expressions hostile. They watched a black girl approach and proposition him. Bolan smiled at the girl and gently refused her services, then he edged around her and walked on. Cars cruised the street. It was apparent that there was commerce here: pimps and pushers, johns and junkies, all drove around looking for a meet. The small-timers loitered, looking for opportunity.

A gaggle of young men staggered toward him, though in the street, not on the sidewalk. They were giggling drunk, and the Executioner guessed they were students. Apple-cheeked boys. The four blacks stared at them with unmixed contempt.

"Hey, uh ..."

A young woman had emerged from the shadow of a tree and was in front of him almost before he noticed her.

"I can give you an awful good time, honey," she said in a low, throaty voice. "No holds barred. Anythin' you want. I mean *anythin'*."

The short blond hooker looked hard and weary. She wore a pair of skimpy white shorts, and her ample breasts were spilling out of a loose, dark blue halter.

"What's your name?" Bolan asked.

"Susan."

"You need a fix pretty bad, don't you, Susan?"

She licked her lips. "Yeah. You figured it. I do need it, mister. I sure do need it. I mean, I'm hurting."

"Where do you get it?"

"Jeez, I can't tell you that! You know I can't talk about that. I mean, what's your angle?"

"I want to make a buy myself," Bolan lied. "I'll buy it. I'll give you some. No cash, Susan. Just some stuff."

She sighed loudly. "The guy'd kill me if he thought I put somebody onto him. I mean, how do I know who you are?"

"The guy's not going to know who put me onto him," Bolan assured her. "You'll be out of sight when I talk to him."

Susan shook her head. "This is crazy. Just let me give you a good time and—"

"No. I need a supplier, too. I've been out of town, and I've got to find somebody."

"Got to?" she asked suspiciously.

"Right. Got to."

She thought about it for a long moment, wetting her lips and sucking deep breaths. "Well... Hey, you...you promise?"

"I promise," he said. "I make a buy, you get some."

She hesitated another moment, then nodded decisively. "Okay. The dude drives a black Mercedes. A big one. He's on the streets. I saw him a little while ago."

"I'll find him."

"Hey..." she called to Bolan's back, trotting after him. "Buy from the dude. Don't buy from some kid. What the dude sells is okay. The kids buy from him, but he doesn't give them a wholesale price. They make their bread by cutting the stuff, and they cut it with anything at all. Never know what you're getting."

"Okay."

"And...and one thing more. What I need is the real shit. I mean, heroin. Not coke."

Bolan nodded.

He returned the way he had come, walking past the four lounging blacks.

"Hey, honk," one of them said. "You wanna nice chick, say the word. But take some advice and keep a distance from sister scumbag back there. She a walkin' ecosystem of microbiology."

"Thanks."

Bolan turned the corner and tried another street, looking for the black Mercedes. He stepped over a derelict lying on the sidewalk—maybe alive, maybe dead. Nobody seemed to care. There were more college boys, more street solicitors, and three times he spotted deals going down. It was probably just as Susan had said—small-timers bought from a pusher and did little deals with users who didn't know the pusher or wouldn't be trusted by him or couldn't wait for him.

It was the same commerce, whether it was big or little. What they were selling was death. But there was no point in slapping down two-bit street sellers. For every one you got rid of, two would step in, glad to take his place.

He spotted the Mercedes, fifty-thousand dollars' worth of car, sitting at the curb under a streetlight, parking lights burning. And a million dollars' worth of cocksure dude inside.

Cocksure and with good reason. Two men were in the car—he had a bodyguard.

And, as Bolan watched, a woman approached the car. He could now watch a deal and be sure, before he moved in on the dealer. The woman—she looked to be about forty, well dressed, attractive—handed something to the man in the front seat, probably her money. He reached out and fondled her breasts. She stiffened, but didn't stop him. Then he grabbed her hand, held it for a moment, then reached out and pressed something into her palm—her package, beyond doubt. The transaction was complete.

The woman hurried away.

Bolan stepped into the street and walked over to the driver's door. The engine was running, and the windows were rolled up. He rapped on the window.

The glass slid down smoothly and a broad, disinterested face looked up at him. The man wore a fuzzy, gray, wide-brimmed hat, a white shirt and tie, a dark blue suit with wide lapels. The toothpick in the corner of his mouth made a small indentation in his lip.

"What you got in mind, daddy?" the man rumbled.

"Need a little stuff," Bolan said. "You got the best. You got the only good stuff on the street."

The man shook his head curtly. "Shee-it. What makes you think I deal?"

"A car like this, in a place like this . . . You're dealing. Anyway, I just watched you do a deal."

The dude glanced over the back of the seat to the man sitting in the rear.

"Roy," the dude drawled, "you happen to have them brass knucks in your pocket?"

Roy grinned and nodded.

"Now, white boy," the dude continued. "You either one of two things. Either you a narc, in which case you about to show me your badge. Or you not, in which case you about to move along before Roy comes out and puts a crease in your skull."

"If I was a narc," Bolan replied, "I'd have enough on you to make the bust. I told you I just saw you deal. But I'm not a narc, and I want to make a buy."

"Roy . . ."

The man in the back seat pulled brass knuckles from a jacket pocket and reached for the door handle.

The dealer in front went for a pistol and had his hand on it before the slug from Bolan's Beretta punched through his skull.

The man in the back seat was in a frenzy, slapping gore off his face and clothes. He looked at Bolan, his eyes wide with terror.

"Roy, I want you to take this message to Cesare," Bolan said. "Tell him the Executioner's in town."

Roy jerked open the door, threw himself out of the vehicle and fell to his knees. He scrambled up and ran into the night.

Bolan looked around and caught sight of Susan.

"You're crazy!" she screamed. "You killed my man! Where'm I going to get my stuff? God!"

"I can get you some help," Bolan offered gently.

Susan dropped to her knees and began to weep.

3

Sometime later a cab dropped Bolan at a brightly lighted motel on Interstate 90. Though it was almost two in the morning, the motel was busy, with a constant stream of cars coming and going. The smoky bar was filled and meals were still being served in the dining room.

The Executioner had changed into a navy blue suit and was carrying a soft leather businessman's overnight case. His Beretta 93-R was nestled in a quick-draw shoulder rig, concealed by the jacket, and the leather bag held a mini-Uzi and several magazines of 9 mm ammo—just in case he needed more firepower than the Beretta could generate. The bag also held the rest of his equipment: black suit, combat boots, grenades—both fragmentation and white phosphorous.

The clerk behind the desk was a wise guy, and had the hardened look of an enforcer. "You got a reservation?" he asked.

"I was told I wouldn't need one. I might not stay all night."

The clerk's eyes rose to stare at him—cold, skeptical, humorless. "Not much of the night left."

"Well, I was told you'd still serve the best dinner that can be had in this town at this hour. Then I could find a little action here."

"Who told you that?"

Bolan shrugged. "Some guy beside me on the late plane from Dallas. Never asked his name, never told him mine. You know how it is on planes."

"Dallas... Yeah. Dallas. What kind of action'd you have in mind?"

"What do you recommend? I'll check with you after I have something to eat."

The clerk nodded and resumed reading his newspaper.

As soon as the elevator doors closed and Bolan was out of sight, the clerk picked up a telephone and pressed some numbers.

"Bernie? Joe. Was there a flight in from Dallas in the last hour or so? I got a guy who checked in who says he was on a flight from Dallas that was late."

He need not have troubled. Bolan had done something similar.

THE ROOM WAS EXACTLY what Bolan had expected—adequate. It had a double bed, a smoky old black-and-white television set and a tiny bathroom with chipped and stained fixtures.

This operation was a gold mine. All you had to do was to walk through the halls to see that it was a cathouse—the traffic was heavy. Somewhere on the premises they were running a gambling casino. That wasn't so obvious; he'd have to talk his way in there. From the sweet smell hanging in the halls, someone—or rather, a lot of someones—were smoking marijuana in the rooms. If that much pot was being smoked, it made sense that it was sold here. And it was likely that other substances were, too.

What interested Bolan more were the management and protection. If so much profitable business was being conducted in the motel, the operation wasn't run by amateurs, nor by low-rank employees. Somewhere in this rattrap there had to be a rat. And with so much money going through the place every night, there had to be a small army of hardmen somewhere nearby.

Bolan's plan was to find the rat. To do that, he'd have to break through the hardmen.

A problem: how to fight a skirmish without hurting the civilians who swarmed the place? They were hardly innocents, but they didn't deserve to die for their vices.

He had told the desk clerk he'd eat dinner before he sampled the action. That meant he had an hour before the clerk would begin to wonder why he didn't show up to ask about the action. An hour to raise another blister on the ass of Cesare Frenchi.

Bolan shoved the overnight bag under the bed. It was possible that they'd check his room, but there was nothing he could do to prevent it. At least he could find out whether someone had entered the room in his absence. Bolan placed markers in the window and door—folded paper matches that someone could stick back in the cracks if they noticed them when they fell, but could never put back exactly in the right position.

With the Beretta 93-R secure in its harness under his arm, Bolan left his room and began a quick but effective recon of the motel. To begin, he took the elevator down to the lobby and made sure the night clerk saw him walk through, as if on his way to the dining room. It was easy enough to walk into the dining room and out the side door without the clerk seeing him.

And, having made that appearance, he had his hour to prowl, to find out just what was going on here.

That the hotel was a whorehouse was nothing special or surprising. No great money was made from prostitution anymore. It was nothing more than a sideline—though as a sideline it could bring in important money when a woman could sell drugs to the johns or lead them into casino rooms. That's how the defilement of young women was worked in Vegas and Atlantic City. Naked bodies on the show stages, and other naked bodies in the bedrooms, lured the big-money suckers. In a place like the motel, it was a come-on, as lively as the trade might appear. Somewhere in the building something was going on that generated a lot more profit.

Bolan walked into the bar. The hookers weren't working there—at least not conspicuously. They were getting their assignments at the desk, not by edging up to customers on the bar stools.

He walked down a first-floor hall, then across a lateral corridor and through a hall that paralleled the first one, back to the front. Nothing but rooms. He did the same on the second floor with the same result, then proceeded to the third.

Pay dirt. A pair of hardmen stood guard.

"Hey," he called, pretending to be slightly drunk.

"Hey," one of the hardmen replied.

Bolan sized them up. The first hardman—the one who had spoken—was armed. He had a distinct bulge under his jacket. But he was a polished wise guy, one who could talk to the casual civilian who wandered along the hall by mistake. The other man was sullen. He kept silent and watched with a threatening, suspicious mien.

"Who do I see 'bout getting in for some of the action?" Bolan asked.

"No action," the hardman said. "What are you talking about?"

"No big deal," Bolan replied, keeping up his pretense of being too drunk for much conversation. "Ol' buddy on the airplane said there was action here. Like to . . . like to put a little down on that there. If you guys... If I got it wrong... Who's the guy to talk to?''

The hardman smiled scornfully. "You got it all wrong, buddy. You lookin' for some action, you might ask the man at the desk. He might be able to tell you where to go."

Bolan grinned foolishly and nodded. "Right. Talk to the man at the desk." He broadened his grin. "So, see you later, fellas."

Good enough. Now he knew where the casino was located. The Executioner was about to crash the party.

THE WARRIOR CHANGED into his blacksuit in his room and donned the harness that held the Beretta. Next he slung the mini-Uzi over his shoulder and clipped several grenades to his web belt. Then he eased open the window and stuck his head out.

Room 284 was toward the rear of the motel, above the parking lot. Bolan's window was outside the bright glare of the lights that illuminated the swimming pool, but a small floodlight mounted on the wall ten feet above him cast a dim yellow glow over the parking lot. Poised on the windowsill outside his room, Bolan took out the light with a shot from the silenced Beretta. He waited to see whether anyone had noticed. When it appeared no one had, he tossed a loop of nylon cord over the dead light, using it as a hook to lift himself from his window to the roof.

The motel was three stories high, topped by a flat roof covered with gravel spread on tar. The cooling tower for the motel air-conditioning stood toward the rear, its fans and pumps roaring.

Bolan padded across the roof to the northwest corner, where he would be directly above the casino. He leaned out and checked the windows just below him—covered. He wouldn't be able to see a thing. Besides, if he went over the ledge to peer into a window, he'd be in full sight of the parking lot.

Crouching, he surveyed the roof. Aside from the cooling tower, there were vent pipes every few yards, as well as air intakes and outlets—fat cylinders with conical caps—and hatches.

Hatches... The nearest one was padlocked, but the warrior pulled a tool from one of the pouches on his web belt and quickly picked the lock. He opened the hatch, which revealed a crawl space between the roof and the ceiling of the third floor—space for ducts, pipes and wiring. He let himself down into the crawl space and closed the hatch. It was dark, but he had a small flashlight.

Bolan inched forward on elbows and knees, and was soon above the room that had to be the casino. The ceiling was solid, and he could hear nothing. But he could see the gleam of light around the edges of the electric junction boxes, where light fixtures were mounted in the ceiling below.

His eyes had adjusted to the darkness of the crawl space, and he switched off the flashlight. He was in the middle of a tangle of ducts. Feeling the thin steel, he could tell which ones carried cool air and which ones were the return ducts. They were sealed to the bodies of the ceiling grates with sticky tape. He pulled the tape off a return duct, which was fastened to the grate with two sheet-metal screws. With the screwdriver blade on his knife, Bolan removed the two screws. Then, carefully, without any noise to reveal his presence, he lifted the duct away from the grate and pushed it to one side.

The crawl space filled with light. Bolan jerked back, realizing that the light coming up through the foot-square grate had struck him full in the face and made him visible to anyone who happened to glance up. He repositioned himself away from the light and stared down into the room.

No one was likely to glance up. The female at the blackjack table directly below was topless, blond, pretty and busty. Sure. She'd distract the suckers from their cards. Topless dealers weren't allowed in legitimate casinos, not out of any moral compunctions on the part of casino commissions, but for the very reason that players lost more to topless dealers—it was regarded as an unfair advantage.

He gazed around the room. There was no roulette table, just two more blackjack tables and two tables for craps. The other dealers were topless, too, as were a couple of girls who carried trays and brought drinks to the players.

The gamblers were playing with chips, but he couldn't see where they bought them. There had to be a bank someplace, and he was interested in finding it.

Bolan crawled to another duct, where he performed the same maneuvers. This time he found the bank, in a small room adjoining the casino room. He watched and listened as a man came in for chips.

"Sit, Mr. Hoperman," said the man behind the desk. "Feel a run of luck comin' on?"

"Could be. My check good?"

"They always have been."

With gray hair and a ruddy face, Hoperman was dressed in a dark brown suit. The man behind the desk was younger, heavier and coarser. He was smoking a cigar, which was by now nothing but a stub.

Hoperman wrote his check. "If one of these ever comes back," he said, "just call me. You're the last guys in the world I'd try to pass a bum check on. If it ever happens, it's a mistake, and I'll make it right the same day."

The man glanced at the check. "Two thou. You want—"

"One thou for chips, one for stuff. I'll pick up the stuff when I cash in for the night."

"It'll be ready."

As soon as Hoperman left the room, the man behind the desk pressed a button. The door opened, and a hardman wearing a tuxedo entered.

"Hoperman."

"I seen 'im," Tuxedo grunted.

"We'll let him lose his thou and pick up his stuff. But you guys be ready. And look, nobody takes the stuff off him. I want it found. A whole thou worth, right?"

"Sure. Right."

"And not before he gets to Quincy. He's got to be found *down there*, and with a lot of stuff on him."

"Right."

"Okay. Those country club sons of bitches mess around again . . . Well, what do you wanna bet they don't?"

As soon as Tuxedo was out the door, the man behind the desk picked up the telephone.

"He's here. It's set. Damn right. Marty's handling it. Don't have to worry. I'll call you when Marty comes back. Okay. Thanks. Be in touch."

While the man was talking, Bolan tried the grate to see whether he could lift it out. It was loose and he pulled hard.

The man looked up as he replaced the telephone receiver. "Hey, what—"

The slug from the Beretta crashed through his mouth, and punched through the back of his skull. He slumped forward over the desk, leaking red all over Hoperman's check.

Bolan replaced the grating, then the duct, and crawled back to the casino room. Play went on. No one had heard the almost silent cough of the Beretta.

But the body in the office would be found soon enough, and it would take no more than five minutes to discover how it had happened. It was time for the Executioner to change clothes again.

WHEN BOLAN REACHED the desk, word hadn't yet reached the clerk that the night boss of the casino was dead.

"Good dinner," the warrior said to the desk clerk he had spoken to before. "So now, can I get in on some action?"

"What kind of action?"

"Personally I favor blackjack."

"Do you know how to keep things to yourself?"

"Oh, sure. I wasn't born yesterday."

"Okay. Here's a card. You go up to the third floor and back to 334. Show this card to the guys at the door."

"Thanks."

Bolan took the elevator to the third floor. Tuxedo's name was Marty, apparently. Maybe, if Hoperman hadn't left yet... When they found the dead man, Marty would have other things to do—things other than hitting Hoperman. And if they hadn't found the body, they would when he, Bolan, came in and wanted to buy chips. If Hoperman hadn't already left, with the hardman following, then the guy had a reprieve.

As Bolan turned the corner into the hall that led to the northwest corner, it was obvious that the body had been discovered. People were shoving their way through the casino door, making down the hall, past Bolan. He'd be okay.

Bolan hurried back to his room to retrieve his leather bag. He carried it down the side stairs and out into the parking lot. Maybe there was more to do here, but it didn't seem a good idea to be in room 284 any longer.

Panic was spreading through the motel. Lights were coming on in rooms that had been dark; people raced into the parking lot and screeched away in their cars. No one wanted to be around when the police arrived.

Bolan looked for Hoperman and Marty. Seeing neither one, he headed toward the rear of the motel. Maybe Marty kept his car in the unlighted lot there. And it was possible that Hoperman parked back there, too, since he came to pick up stuff.

As he reached the back of the building, the warrior spotted Marty.

And one of his guesses had been right—Marty had something on his mind besides hitting Hoperman. He hurried across the parking lot to a big Buick station wagon, carrying two canvas bags. Two hardmen guarded the station wagon. Marty barked something at them, and one man stepped smartly to open the rear hatch. Marty heaved in the canvas bags and trotted back toward the motel.

Another tuxedo-clad man left the building, carrying an attaché case and a leather suitcase. These, too, went into the back of the station wagon.

Okay, it made sense. The cops were coming. Too many people in the casino had seen the corpse through the door, and somebody was sure to call the police. These guys were carrying out the stuff—cocaine for sure, heroin probably, amphetamines maybe. Bolan guessed that the attaché case and suitcase were filled with cash.

Two more men came out carrying the crap tables, and shoved them into the back of a van parked next to the station wagon. Then they got in the van and drove off. They didn't need to bring down the blackjack tables; those were just ordinary tables and weren't evidence of illegal gambling.

Marty appeared with two more canvas bags. He was sweating and puffing. "That's it," Bolan heard him say to the two hardmen. "Be right back. No touch."

He raced back to the motel. One of the hardmen lit a cigarette and lounged against the station wagon. The other stood a little apart, looking around.

Bolan put down his leather bag, opened it and removed two grenades, one frag, one phosphorous. Then he withdrew the mini-Uzi from the bag and catfooted toward the station wagon, shielding himself with a row of cars. When he was fifty feet from the vehicle he decided to see how much courage the two hardmen had. Taking aim over the hood of a car, he fired a burst from the Uzi into the side windows of their Buick.

No courage. They took off running.

Bolan sprinted over to the wagon, pulled the pin from his phosphorous grenade and tossed it among the canvas bags Marty had piled in the back. As the warrior raced away to duck behind a car, the grenade went off. The white-hot phosphorous incinerated everything in the station wagon—money, cocaine, heroin—before the fire even reached the gas tank. The station wagon exploded in a ball of yellow flame.

4

Cesare Frenchi lay in the swirling hot water of a Jacuzzi, but he wasn't relaxed.

"What do you mean, *phosphorous*?" he shouted into the telephone that was jammed to his ear. "You're *dead*, is what you are! You're a dead man, Marty! You can't run far enough or fast enough that I won't—"

He looked up at the two bewildered girls who had been rubbing him with bath oil before the call came. "Out! Out! Out!" he yelled. They scrambled to their feet and ran, closing the bathroom door behind them.

"You loaded every goddamn thing you had into one goddamn car? Well, nobody ever said you were bright, Marty."

He gave the stub of his strong, thin cigar a furious toss toward the toilet. It missed and bounced against the wall, showering sparks onto the floor.

Frenchi was in his early thirties, paunchy, slack-muscled and bald, though his body was abundantly hairy. He had never grown much beyond the five foot five that in school had earned him the nickname Little Caesar—a nickname no one dared use now. His head and face were small, and his little brown eyes glared at the world from under heavy black eyebrows. Even in the bath he wore an expensive gold watch and, on his left hand, a gold pinkie ring set

with a huge glittering diamond. His fingernails were man-
icured daily and coated with clear lacquer, his toes, weekly.

"What do you mean it was Henry's idea? Oh . . . 'His
evacuation plan.' You can't lie to me, Marty. You can lie
to your mother easier than you can lie to me. Henry . . .
Hey, you sure you didn't shoot him yourself?"

He settled back in the water, holding the phone away
from his ear as the frightened Marty pleaded.

The trouble was, how could he know how much went up
in smoke in that station wagon? How could he know that
son of a bitch Marty and his buddies didn't kill Henry
and—

"How much stuff was in there, Marty? How much
money? How much . . . ? Shit! I'll tell you one thing, you
bastard. You better be poor. You better be poor for the rest
of your life, or I'll know you wasted Henry and ripped off
half of what was supposed to be in that station wagon."

He threw a bar of soap at the door. One of the girls
opened it cautiously and peered inside. He swung his arm
to order her back in and pointed at the cigar. Then at the
bath oil. She picked up the wet butt and dropped it in the
toilet, then knelt by the tub and began to rub the oil over
Cesare's shoulders.

"Two guys. Two guys busted and ran. Well, I'll tell you
what, Marty. You want to save your balls? Then deliver me
theirs. Both guys. Before noon. How can we operate if
men left to take care of something bust and run at the first
sound of a shot? Before noon, Marty. Then you get out to
Quincy and waste Hoperman. And do somethin' right for
once! You want the Don's place in this organization? Well,
you aren't going to get it. But if you want to live to wish
you had it, you get on the stick, Marty."

Cesare slammed down the receiver.

CESARE FRENCHI HAD BEEN a boy when Mack Bolan ruined everything. All his life he'd heard that name, and now some son of a bitch wanted him to believe Bolan had come to Boston.

That was a sick joke. Somebody knew how to get to him. The son of a bitch who had shot the dealer called himself the Executioner and had sent the dealer's sidekick with the word.

"Padrino..." the girl murmured. She wanted to suggest he lean forward so that she could rub the oil on his back. He understood and bent over. *"Molte grazie,"* she whispered.

He glanced at the girl, whose name was Clara. She was newly arrived from Sicily—a cute, fat, innocent eighteen-year-old. Her family was in trouble with the Honored Society back in Palermo, and they had sent her over here. With a dowry. He was supposed to find her a husband. Okay, he would. In the meantime she was glad to be taught a few wifely skills.

Cesare Frenchi remembered the days before Bolan. The Men of Respect had come to the house in a constant stream, kissing his father's hand when he greeted them, bringing him gifts, tokens of their esteem—and often bringing gifts for his mother and for himself and his brothers and sisters. Cesare had accumulated more boyhood treasures than he could possibly use—six or seven bicycles, as many sleds, electric trains of all kinds, toy soldiers, plus footballs, basketballs, baseballs and bats, gloves, games, knives, BB guns...

His mother had suggested just once that some of these gifts should be given away to families who couldn't afford such things for their children. Cesare's father, Sergio Frenchi, told her with finality that *nothing* was to be given away. Nothing. Giving away an item would dishonor the man who had brought it to the house. What was more, Cesare and the other children should remember who gave them what and be seen playing with the appropriate gift when the giver came to the house.

In any case, Cesare would have resisted giving anything away. By nature he was what some would have called acquisitive, others greedy. He had hoarded his treasures. He compared them with what his brothers had, and if he saw that a brother had more—say, one more bicycle than he had—he would close himself in his room and cry. Furthermore, if he knew who had given his brother something and hadn't given him as much, he resented that man.

Cesare had a long memory. To this day he was hostile to the sons of Dominic Petricone because Petricone had given his brother Vinnie an American Flyer train set and hadn't given anything to little brother Cesare. It had made no difference in Cesare's thinking that Vinnie was Petricone's godson. He had sneaked into the cellar where his brother had set up the train and broken the locomotive with a hammer. But that was his revenge on Vinnie. He still looked for ways to hurt the Petricones.

When Cesare was nine, Mack Bolan had begun to make war on the Family. Cesare hadn't understood what was going on. He understood only that his father had sent him away to a boarding school, called Deerfield Academy, in the western part of the state.

His father might as well have sent him to hell. For starters, to the other prep-school boys, Cesare Frenchi was inevitably "Little Caesar." What was worse, he was nobody. The Men of Respect didn't bear gifts to Deerfield Academy. No one kissed anyone's hand at Deerfield, and if they had, it wouldn't have been the hand of the aggressive, foul-mouthed little Italian kid from Boston. At Deerfield, Cesare Frenchi had been just another boy, with nothing special to distinguish him, and he had been expected to conform to the mores and standards of the school.

After six weeks the headmaster had called Sergio Frenchi to Deerfield for a conference. Following that meeting, the father sat with the boy in an armored black Cadillac and explained to him that the Family was under attack, that he was here for his safety, that Deerfield was a fine school and he was privileged to be there—and if he made any more trouble, his father would bring him home, take down his pants and put welts on his bottom that would sting for the rest of his life.

Cesare had stayed at Deerfield for eight miserable years. He had no option. His father was dead, his mother had fled to Sicily, taking his sisters with her and his brothers were scattered among other prep schools and colleges. There was no longer any family home, and he had nowhere to go. There had been money, though. Men of Respect had paid his tuition and expenses, and had sent him envelopes containing hundred-dollar bills. His father had arranged that. It was a debt of honor, payable to Cesare, and it was paid.

When he was fourteen, he killed a boy named McIntyre. For five years McIntyre had done everything he could to hurt and humiliate Cesare Frenchi. Cesare had waited patiently for his chance, and finally the opportunity had come. McIntyre had stepped out onto a fire escape platform to smoke—strictly a violation of the rules—and, as Cesare had seen him do many nights, he had sat on the railing, idly dangling his feet, his back to a thirty-foot drop onto a sidewalk below. It had been especially simple since it would never enter the minds of the innocents at Deerfield that one of the boys would actually kill another.

The death of McIntyre had given Cesare new self-respect and self-confidence, and he liked the feeling. He had rehearsed the murder many nights in bed, and after he had done it, he reviewed it night after night. The only thing that could have made the incident more satisfying for Cesare would have been for the other boys to know, or at least to suspect, what he had done. Then they would have understood that Cesare Frenchi was *somebody*.

He had resented everything about the academy, but he stayed there, did enough studying to avoid boredom and graduated with honors. What else could he have done? That was what his father had provided for, and he'd had no place else to go. Cesare never heard from his brothers. They didn't care about him, and he sure didn't give a damn about them. He had received two letters from his mother during all those years. He didn't give a damn about that, either.

During the fall of his final year at Deerfield, Enrico "Henry" Romeo had come to the academy with word that Sergio had provided money for his son to go to Harvard. He should apply. The university knew the money was available.

What if he didn't want to go to Harvard? Romeo had shrugged. That was what his father had wanted.

Henry Romeo had become his friend, his first real friend among connected men. The relationship had lasted until last night, when someone put a bullet through Henry's head.

Cesare's father, and the Men of Respect who had carried out his father's trust, had expected the young man to study business administration, or maybe law. The Families recognized a growing need for men with education. The world was changing and the old ways of making a living had become more difficult. Foreigners were moving in—Hispanics into the drug business, for example. The states themselves sold numbers now, which just about ruined that easy source of income. Competition from amateurs, plus the fear of disease, had hurt prostitution. And so on. Some of the New York Families had almost completely left the traditional lines and were making their money in banking, insurance, real estate—all kinds of endeavors that used to be strictly straight. Cesare Frenchi would learn all about those kinds of businesses and would become a valuable man.

His brothers had. Vinnie Frenchi was *consigliere* to a Los Angeles Don.

But Cesare's father hadn't known his son.

Cesare was a man without patience. Shortly after he was enrolled as a Harvard freshman and installed in a small Cambridge apartment, he was running two Radcliffe girls. It had been a convenient arrangement for all three: Cesare had wanted to make his start in business, and the two girls had been desperate for money. Sara had a habit and needed fifty dollars a day. Linda had been into a loan shark for a thousand.

Six weeks after Cesare began to run Linda, her shark had leaned on her, bruised her face and made her unavailable to earn money for two weeks. Cesare had a short fuse and was partial to simple, final solutions. In a Cambridge alley he had driven a knife into the hood's back. Fourteen times.

The man had been connected, but no one had known who hit him. Certainly no one had suspected the Frenchi kid, the college boy, which was lucky for Cesare—and too bad. Once again he had killed, and once again he couldn't advertise.

Sara was the last person with a habit who Cesare ever allowed to work for him. She couldn't be trusted, even to keep her mouth shut. When a student in one of his classes approached Cesare and asked how much he would charge for a whole weekend with Linda, he had only shrugged and laughed, as if the idea were too ridiculous to discuss. Two days later he murdered Sara.

Within a year he had eight girls on the street. That brought him to the attention of a black pimp, who tried to muscle in on him. The guy became the fourth person killed by Cesare Frenchi.

Within the same year he branched out. He wanted to start a small gambling room, and you couldn't do that without the permission of the local boss. Henry Romeo told him who to see.

Who to see was Ramondo Grotteria, which couldn't have been better, since Grotteria was one of the trustees of the fund the late Sergio Frenchi had left for the education of his sons. Grotteria was distressed to learn that Cesare had elected to be made as soon as possible instead of continuing the education Sergio had wanted for him. On the other hand Ramondo Grotteria was a practical man.

Cesare told him to take whatever money was left in his father's fund, as a gift, as a mark of respect. He told Grotteria he was running some girls and wanted to open a gambling operation, small at first, maybe something better as time went on. He would, of course, pay Grotteria the usual percentage—and ten percent more. And . . . and he had to make a confession. He had hit the loan shark. Also the pimp. Cesare wanted to start with everything above-board.

Grotteria had made him, then and there. That is, he had made him a member of the Mafia, of the Grotteria Family. Cesare had declared his gratitude to Grotteria and pledged him loyalty.

His loyalty had lasted a little less than five years.

CESARE CALLED for Bonnie, and she returned to the bathroom. Clara, from Sicily, remained a virgin, technically, and he meant to keep her that way. He had, after all, promised to marry her to someone, and it wouldn't be good politics to offer a man shopworn merchandise—not to mention how her family in Sicily would react. He had no such problem with Bonnie and curtly ordered her into the tub.

Bonnie was a good girl. She'd done seven years for manslaughter; her boyfriend had pulled life. He was dead now, killed in a knife fight in the pen. Maybe a straight beef, maybe not. The trouble was, the truck driver they'd killed while trying to pull a hijacking had been a made man. Not only had two dumb kids tried a caper like that in Al Felucci's town, but they'd killed one of his soldiers. Bonnie was under Cesare's protection; she needed it. She was also under his thumb. A good deal, all the way around.

Someone knocked on the door.

"Yeah?"

"Sal Balestrino is on the phone."

Cesare shook his head and reached for the telephone. Balestrino was his pencil pusher. If anyone knew just how much went up in smoke last night, Sal would.

"Hey, Sally. What's the bad news?"

Balestrino had been hit across the throat with a baseball bat in a rumble many years ago, and he spoke with a ravaged voice. You had to listen carefully to be able to understand him. "We lost a million bucks last night, Cesare," he croaked. "I figure a million and about forty thou. That'd be about eight hundred fifty thou's worth of stuff—the coke, the crack, the shit, a few pills. And the rest in cash. Hey, that's not all. There had to be checks.

Henry took checks. Not much in checks in the house, I don't figure. What . . . ? Maybe ten. Fifteen at the most."

"Eight-fifty . . . ?"

"Selling value. We're out maybe a hundred seventy-five, cash laid out for the stuff."

"Damn!"

"Yeah . . . Somebody hit us hard. Damn hard. Plus of course, Henry. You don't find many guys like Enrico Romeo. Tough damn—"

"Yeah, *yeah*. Okay, Sal. Look, I gotta think. Be here at three, like I said."

Cesare put the phone down beside the 7.65 mm Walther PPK that was never beyond his reach.

Yeah, he had to think.

This was too much like what he'd heard of—that crazy guy Bolan coming on with military-type weapons and slaughtering people like so many animals. If Bolan was in town, he was working the same way. A phosphorous grenade, for God's sake? And the soldiers had run off because they heard—or said they heard—a burst from an automatic weapon.

A million *and* Henry! Also—what the hell—the street pusher, though he had to admit Jackson DeWitt had been a good merchant, putting out more than three or four other guys. Both Henry and DeWitt with a hole through the head, and both in one night.

Well, if war was what they wanted, war was what they'd get.

AT THREE O'CLOCK Frenchi sat at the head of a table in the conference room of his penthouse suite. He was dressed conservatively in a gray suit, white shirt, red-and-blue striped necktie. The PPK hung at his armpit, as always when he was dressed.

The seat to his right was vacant. It was Enrico Romeo's. Marty Luchese sat in the chair next to it. The rough, fat man was uncomfortable, sweating. To Cesare's left sat Salvatore Balestrino, an older man who was still big and rugged. To Balestrino's left was Guido Terranova, a dark man—dark of complexion, dark of mien—in his thirties. He had about him the menacing look appropriate to what he was—the Frenchi enforcer.

The remaining seats around the table, four of them, were occupied by Cesare Frenchi's button men. Marty Luchese was a button man, as well.

"Okay, Marty," Cesare began. "Report."

"What you said, you got," Luchese said quietly.

"The two soldiers?"

Luchese nodded. "With the fishes."

"Hoperman?"

"Turn on your radio."

"All right," Cesare said. "Now... Sally says we lost more than a million dollars last night. Who hit us?"

The button men—lieutenants—shook their heads.

"Could it have been Mack Bolan?" Cesare asked.

"Hey," mumbled one of the button men, Antonio Venosa. "You sayin' that guy's *real*?"

"Real," Cesare replied. "And the guy who shot Jackson DeWitt last night said he was Bolan. Sent the word to me—the Executioner's in town."

"Why? Hasn't he got anything better to do?"

"The problem," Sally growled in his measured, gravelly voice, "is that you guys hit an Uncle Sugar. The guy at Dundee was—"

"A plant," Venosa said.

"Uncle Sugar, just the same," Sal continued. "When you hit the government, you bring down heat. Big heat."

"They don't come any bigger," Cesare responded. "That is, if we got Bolan in town."

"We're gonna have peace to make," Sal told them. "That guy is bad news, and if we brought him to town, a lotta guys are gonna be pissed."

"Sally," Cesare said firmly, "I don't give a damn who's pissed. And there's only one way to handle this—the way the old man should have done and saved the world a lot of trouble."

"Hit Bolan," Terranova suggested.

"It's not that easy," Cesare said. "And it's not that simple. But I got an idea. The Sugar we hit was named El- liott—Ron Elliott. He was from Baltimore. That's Sesto- la's territory, right?"

Sal nodded. "Sestola . . ."

"I want a sitdown with Sestola," Cesare told him. "I'll fly down there. Tomorrow would be a good time. Call the guy, Sally. I want a sitdown with Sestola."

5

Special Agent DiRosario sat across the table from Mack Bolan in the coffee shop of the Hyatt Regency Hotel in Cambridge.

"You've seen the papers?" he asked.

Bolan nodded.

The morning edition of the *Globe* featured a front-page picture of the burned-out hulk of the Buick station wagon. The accompanying story guessed pretty accurately what had happened.

Burned in the white-hot heat of what fireman say must have been a phosphorous grenade was an immense amount of cash that appears to have been inside two briefcases, plus a large quantity of cocaine and heroin. Police say they have as yet no clue as to who owned the station wagon, but theorize that it belonged to a narcotics dealer and was burned by a rival.

Friends of Enrico Romeo, the man shot and killed inside the motel, say they have no idea what might have motivated his killing. "Henry had been in the motel business all his life," said one. "So far as I know, he didn't have an enemy in the world."

"When you hit town, you hit town!" DiRosario marveled. Considering what had gone down, Brognola had thought it prudent to let the FBI agents know "Major Morrison's" true identity.

"Cesare Frenchi knows I'm here," Bolan said.

"There's a contract out on you. One million cash, to the guy who can prove he did it. Half a million to anyone who fingers you so Frenchi's hit man can get to you."

Bolan shrugged. "I've been the target of richer contracts than that."

"Well, look." DiRosario glanced around the room, as if to be sure no one was watching them. "The word to Lindsay and me is to give you every kind of cooperation. I don't have to be talked into that. But . . . Well, listen . . . I've got to give you some information, something that's a deep, dirty secret. At least one life is—"

"Tell me or don't," Bolan growled. "You don't have to brief me on keeping secrets."

"Sorry. I, uh . . . Okay. I've got a mole inside Frenchi's organization. Somebody damned close to him. I've arranged a meet. Every meet with me is dangerous, so I've set this up for you alone. Unless you want to call it off."

"When and where?"

BOLAN WAS TO MEET the woman shortly after noon on a bench in a park overlooking the Charles River. Two crews were rowing their racing shells on the river, and the warrior sat and watched while he waited. The coxswains barked their orders and the straining rowers grunted, the seats in the shells clacking loudly as they moved back and forth on each stroke.

An ordinary-looking young woman, about thirty years old, dressed in blue jeans and a sweater sat down beside the warrior without a word.

He glanced at her. "Bonnie?"

She nodded.

They sat there in silence for a few moments. The woman's name was Bonnie Hennings and she was DiRosario's mole inside the Frenchi organization—in fact, inside the Frenchi household. She wasn't exceptionally brave, DiRosario had said, and she wasn't particularly smart, but she was all the spy he had. Her motive for taking on the high-risk assignment was her obsessive hatred for Cesare Frenchi. She despised the man; she loathed him.

She and her husband, John, had tried to pull off a truck hijacking years earlier, and they had killed the driver. John had been sentenced to life; Bonnie was allowed to cop a plea of manslaughter and got a ten-to-twenty. She did seven years. Even though Bonnie and John were in prison, Al Felucci had put out contracts on them. John was stabbed to death in the Massachusetts Penitentiary. Bonnie was attacked in the women's penitentiary but fought off her attacker and survived. When she was released, she knew enough to ask for protection and she got it from Cesare Frenchi—but at a price. He owned her.

Long imprisonment puts a mark on convicts. You can see it on someone who has spent a lot of time behind bars—something hard to define but unmistakable, in their skin, in their muscle tone, in the way they walk and sit. Bonnie was subtly marked the same way. She lit a cigarette, and she held it between her thumb and four fingers, as if she had to hide it, or as if she thought someone might try to snatch it from her. What was more, she smoked as if smoking satisfied a hunger.

Otherwise, she wasn't unattractive. Her features were regular, except for her shiny, pouting lower lip, which defined something in her personality—maybe a suppressed longing to laugh and smile more than her circumstances had ever allowed. Her eyes were blue and she wore her mousy, straight hair in a simple bob that fell just below her ears. Heavy bangs covered her forehead, down to her eyebrows.

"They figure you cost them a million dollars," she said quietly. "Street value of what you burned up in that station wagon. Every wise guy in New England, Frenchi's people and everybody else, wants your head. They know who you are." She smiled. "Which is funny. Uncle Sugar had given me the name Morrison—Major Morrison."

"Do they have any idea what I look like, where to find me?" Bolan asked.

She shook her head. "Not yet. You wouldn't be sitting here if they did."

"Who do I have to watch out for most?"

She shrugged. "You ever hear of a guy called Terrible Terranova?"

Bolan shook his head.

"Well, he's the Frenchi enforcer. Guido Terranova. And all he's got to do now, his only assignment, is to hunt you down and kill you."

"Okay."

She glanced up into his face. "Hey, Bolan, I hear you're a tough man. I hear you cut a swath through these guys a long time ago. Well, don't think they're the same kind. Let me tell you something. Cesare Frenchi thinks his father was a Mustache Pete. He's not cut from the same cloth. None of them are. They're smarter and tougher. The old guys...there was a kind of honor with them. Not this crowd. There are no rules."

"Tell me about Cesare Frenchi. What kind of man is he?"

Bonnie stiffened as she drew a deep breath and straightened her back. "He's a *bastard*!" she whispered.

"To you, personally?"

She sighed. "Do you understand what I am? Look, I'm a slave. That's what I am. He *owns* me because Al Felucci has a contract out on me. He had my husband killed, and he wants me. That's the way these guys work. I mean, by keeping people afraid. Terrified. My husband and I were dumb. We tried to hijack a truckload of radios and TV sets. We didn't know it was Felucci's or that the driver was a member of his Family. But didn't know didn't matter. Anybody who steps on Felucci's toes is dead. And I'm dead the minute Frenchi takes his protection off me."

"He keeps you alive."

She nodded. "And, man, does he ever take advantage of it," she added bitterly.

Bolan frowned. "Sexual abuse?"

She nodded.

"Tell me about Felucci."

"Springfield," she said. "He's got a grip on that town like Frenchi doesn't have on Boston. I mean, there are other Families in Boston. There's just one in Springfield. Felucci."

"How'd you get in touch with Cesare Frenchi?" Bolan asked.

"Framingham. The Massachusetts slammer for women. His sister's there, doing twenty-five to life for murdering her husband. Cesare goes to see her every two to three months."

"I thought his sisters were in Sicily."

"Not Nina. She married over there, and her husband brought her to Boston. He was an abusive bastard, and she killed him. Cesare's mother is still living, and she's in Sicily with his other sisters. But poor Nina has ten or twelve years to go before she can get her first parole hearing. Anyway, she and I got to be friends at Framingham, and she set it up for me to go under her brother's protection."

"I'm really interested in the murder of Ron Elliott. What do you know about that?"

"He's responsible," she said flatly. "I heard some talk about killing a Sugar, and how they shouldn't have killed a Sugar. DiRosario told me—"

"Air cargo...?"

"That's what did *me* in," she admitted. "That load of TV sets was stolen from an air-freight warehouse at Hartford." She sighed. "You know, I guess Johnny knew it. I think so now. I think he figured he could steal from somebody who'd stolen it to begin with."

"So Felucci's an air-cargo hijacker, too."

"Felucci's into everything," she told him. "Like I told you, he's got his hooks into that part of the state. And across the line, too, into Connecticut. He brings in coke and heroin through Bradley International, the Hartford airport. The stuff's inside air-cargo crates, and his guys rip it off before customs inspectors can get a look. The Sugars at Hartford think they're tryin' to stop guys from evading import taxes. They don't seem to know that what's coming in is—"

"Death."

"Yeah, right. Three-quarters of the women at Framingham were in there because of something about drugs— what they did to get their fixes, mostly. And they were the lucky ones. A lot of others died—I mean, died on bad stuff, of overdoses... Some of those women had kids who'd been *born* hooked.

"Even inside the joint, they shoot up or sniff stuff," Bonnie continued. "I saw it all the time while I was in the penitentiary." She sighed. "I thank God I never got hooked. It's the only dumb thing I never did do, I guess."

"Okay. I've got a job to do, Bonnie. Are you going to keep on helping?"

She shrugged. "What other chance do I have? I mean, what other chance do I have of breaking loose from Cesare Frenchi?" She shook her head. "As long as he lives... And the guy has a long memory."

Bolan's chin rose. "In other words, you'd like me to kill Felucci and Frenchi?"

"Both of them got it comin'," she said grimly. "What they do to people...it's a crime."

"Where's Frenchi now?"

"He went to Baltimore," she said.

"When are you expected back?"

"Oh... Only when he's back. Tomorrow. I'm let out on a leash when he's out of town."

"How'd you like to show me around Springfield?" Bolan asked.

Her eyes narrowed. "You mean...?"

"You still know your way around?"

"I know."

"I work unofficially," he said. "I could use a tour guide."

Bonnie grinned. "Yeah! Why the hell not? Maybe I can get my life back, huh? Maybe, sooner or later."

BOLAN AND BONNIE checked into the Northampton Hilton Inn, twenty miles or so north of Springfield—a comfortable little mountain resort motel. Bolan had talked with DiRosario and Lindsay before he left Boston, and asked them to confirm or deny Bonnie's description of Alfredo Felucci, which they did.

Al controlled western Massachusetts and a slice of Connecticut with a heavy hand the Five Families in New York would no longer have dared to wield. He still managed to keep a firm hand on the narcotics trade, partly by making shrewd deals with the Hispanics who wanted to move in and partly by killing—families and all—anyone who tried to muscle in. At a time when prostitution no longer counted for much, Felucci still ran at least two hundred girls and made a fat profit. He controlled the construction unions in most towns and invested union pension funds in his own enterprises. He was no minor-league loan shark. To the contrary, many prominent men in his territory owned their homes or businesses through low-interest loans from Felucci, who, in return for his favor and his forbearance from foreclosing, owned these politicians and businessmen in almost the same way that Cesare Frenchi owned Bonnie Hennings. He controlled gambling, hijackings, and, as the two FBI men had put it, Al had a far better grip on his territory than Al Capone had ever had on his.

"All I want you to do," Bolan told Bonnie as he changed clothes in their room at the Hilton Inn, "is to show me Felucci's place. Then you can drive back here, give me, say, an hour and a half, then come back for me."

During the drive west she had told him about Felucci's country house, which was where Bolan had decided to start. If he didn't find Felucci there, at least he would give him something to worry about.

"No way. I'm goin' all the way with you, Bolan."

"Look. This is—"

"A man's work," she interrupted. "The hell it is. Anyway, you're gonna need somebody—at least for a lookout, if nothing more. Besides, I'm not good at pacing the floor in a motel room, waiting to see—"

"Then you'll do as I say if you go with me," he stated firmly.

"Sure. I'm good at that."

"All right. When I tell you to stay back—"

"I stay back. Okay. But—" she pointed at the pistols he was carrying in his suitcase "—you gotta let me carry one of those. I mean, you know, I might have to defend myself."

"You know about the Massachusetts gun law?" he asked.

"Sure. Crooks can have all the guns they want. If an honest citizen is caught with one, he does a year in the slammer."

Bolan grinned. That expressed his judgment of the gun laws of Massachusetts and New York. But Bonnie faced a grim problem. "If I let you carry a gun tonight, and you get caught, you could do a lot of time—with your record."

"I'll take my chances."

Bolan offered her a 7.65 mm Walther PPK, a pistol she recognized immediately as the same weapon Cesare Frenchi always kept within reach. Well, she knew Cesare always wanted the best.

The PPK was small, pocket-size—this one a dull, metallic color. She couldn't help but reflect on the contrast between this sophisticated German pistol and the primitive nickel-plated .38 revolvers she and Johnny had carried when they tried their heist. As well, this pistol had a sound-suppressor screwed into the barrel. It hadn't been manufactured this way but had been modified by someone who worked with Bolan. He had explained, too, that it would fire subsonic cartridges, so the sound it would make if she found it necessary to put a bullet in someone would be nothing more than a quiet pop. He gave her two extra clips of ammunition.

"You have to wear something dark," he said. "Your jeans are okay, but not the sweater. Here's a black sweatshirt. It'll fit like a tent, but it's all I've got."

Bolan was carrying heavy artillery. Bonnie knew a little about firearms and knew that a .44 Magnum could blow a fist-sized hole in a man. She knew that a .44 Magnum cartridge—even bigger than the legendary .357 Magnum—was usually fired in a revolver. But Bolan was hanging an *automatic* in the harness he would strap on when after they left the motel.

"What the hell is that?" she asked.

He slipped the big automatic smoothly into its holster. "A Desert Eagle. Let's go."

"I DIDN'T PROMISE that he'd be here," she whispered. "Hell, he might be in the Bahamas."

Bolan nodded.

They were on a wooded slope, two hundred yards above the edge of the Felucci horse farm. The sun had set behind the mountains, though a dull glow still reddened the sky and afforded them a good look at the fenced grounds—which didn't look like much. The godfathers had learned a bitter lesson—that the Internal Revenue Service looked at your house—so shrewd men didn't spend conspicuously. Still, the Felucci estate spoke of comfort, the kind of comfort a man who paid the taxes Felucci paid might afford.

Alfredo Felucci kept a small house and a few acres with a paddock holding no more than three or four horses. The single-story, white frame house looked like a modest ranch house. There were two frame outbuildings: a stable and a solid, concrete-block building.

Bolan studied the white board fence through binoculars, seeing no evidence of sensors. Apparently the place wasn't protected by an electronic alarm, though, as the red sunset faded, floodlights came on, filling the grounds with a bright glare that looked oddly green as contrasted with the glow of the setting sun.

Three cars were parked between the house and the concrete-block building—two big Mercedes sedans and a Porsche 911. He guessed the sedans were armored.

Bonnie nudged his arm, pointing to a man who had just come out of the concrete-block building.

"What's he carrying?" she asked.

Bolan studied him through the binoculars and saw what she meant—the man wore a shoulder holster filled with a big pistol, probably a .357 Magnum.

The man leaned against the wall of the building and lit a cigarette.

"Felucci's inside," Bonnie whispered.

"What makes you think so?"

"He doesn't let anybody smoke around him. The guy wanted a smoke, so he had to go out. It doesn't *prove* he's in there, but—"

Another man left the concrete-block building.

"Take a look at this guy." Bolan handed her the binoculars.

She squinted through the glasses for a moment. "That's Felucci," she confirmed, handing the glasses back.

Bolan watched the man walk to the house. Al weighed in at two-fifty at the very least and he was bald, with gray hair around the sides and back of his head. He stopped to say something to the man with the cigarette, and Bolan could see him making choppy gestures, obviously laying down the law. The man nodded and tossed away his cigarette. Felucci went on talking and gesturing, then suddenly turned and walked toward the house.

"Is Felucci married?" Bolan asked.

"Used to be," Bonnie replied. "His wife died of cancer. They had no children."

"So there's no family in the house."

She shook her head. "Not real family."

"Okay. Let's move in a little closer."

They moved down the slope to the edge of the tree line. By now it was almost dark, and the two black-clad figures were all but invisible to sentries on the brightly lighted grounds. From the look of the place, Felucci depended for his protection on nothing more sophisticated than his thugs.

There were at least two men, and undoubtedly more. A second hardman had come out of the building and joined the first one for a smoke. He wore a shoulder holster and carried a sawed-off shotgun, an evil-looking weapon that he leaned against the wall to free both hands for lighting his cigarette. At his distance Bolan could study their faces through his binoculars. The new man's was deeply pitted with acne scars.

"You stay here," Bolan whispered to his companion. "If the action heats up, try to get a shot into those guys. Even if you miss, you'll distract them."

Bonnie shook her head. "I couldn't do you any good from here. I'll come with you as far as the fence, to the edge of the light."

"I thought you were good at taking orders?" He began to crawl forward, followed by the woman.

The warrior guessed there would be at least one more hardman inside the house with Felucci, maybe two, and there could be others in the concrete-block building. If he got inside the house and hell broke loose, the two he could see would make a dash for the house. Could Bonnie take them out? He doubted it. And what if there were more of them? One small pistol, in the hands of an amateur... Not good odds.

"No heroics," he whispered. "With that silencer in place, they don't know where your shots are coming from. So hug the ground and fire carefully—if you have to fire. Don't stand up."

"Don't worry about that, boss."

"All right. I'm going to try to get into the house. I—"

Bolan suddenly put a hand on the back of Bonnie's head, pushed her face to the grass and dived to the ground beside her. A beam of light swept toward them.

"Headlights," she muttered. "Nothin' but damn headlights."

He raised his head. She was right. They had been caught for a brief moment in the glare of the headlights of a small van that had slowed and turned into the Felucci estate.

The van stopped beside the other vehicles, facing the wall of the concrete-block building. The doors opened, and the driver and another man got out. They walked to the rear of the van and jerked open the double doors.

"All right. Out, you two," the driver barked.

Bolan and Bonnie were close enough to hear the conversation and see the utter terror on the faces of the young man and woman who stumbled out of the van. Their hands were cuffed behind them, and they were gagged. Their eyes were wide, their faces flushed.

Felucci came out of the house. "Well, well," he sneered. "If it ain't Jack and Jill. Nice work, boys."

The capo dug into a pocket of his slacks and pulled out a wad of cash. He peeled off several bills and handed the money to the driver, curtly jerking his thumb over his shoulder. The driver and his companion saluted, then returned to the van. In another moment they were gone, speeding back down the road.

The girl dropped to her knees in front of Felucci. She was crying and tried desperately to mumble a plea through the rag stuffed in her mouth and bound there with a piece of rope.

"That's too damned bad," Felucci snarled. "You should have thought of it before."

Bonnie nudged Bolan, put her mouth to his ear and whispered, "They're gonna kill them!"

Bolan nodded. He'd already drawn the .44 and was attaching the fourteen-inch barrel for a long shot. The distance wasn't so great, but the added accuracy could count for a lot. He leveled the pistol in both hands and sighted on Felucci.

"Nick?" Felucci asked.

The acne-scarred man picked up the sawed-off shotgun. "Who's first?" he asked coldly.

The girl threw herself facedown on the ground and screamed through her gag. The young man stood with his head down, his shoulders heaving with quiet sobs.

"Her. She's too noisy," Felucci said.

The gunman stepped toward the girl, slipped his finger through the trigger guard and seized the barrel tightly in his left hand. Then he exploded. Bolan's .44 Magnum slug shattered his sternum, the pressures it generated inside his rib cage bursting his heart and lungs as the big bullet blew out through his back, spraying bone fragments and gore onto the nearest Mercedes. He was lifted off his feet by the impact and thrown to the ground like a broken doll.

The other gunman threw himself onto the dirt and rolled under the Mercedes, his clothes soaking up his companion's blood. He pulled his revolver from his holster as he rolled, and in the shelter of the car above him he waved the pistol from side to side, searching for a target.

Bolan fired twice, knowing his slugs would chop the ground and ricochet, probably harmlessly, under the car. One struck a bit of rock and spun upward, puncturing the door of the Mercedes, and the other crashed into a part of the undercarriage. The two shots served their purpose, though—the gunman scooted backward, trying to put more heavy steel between him and the powerful rounds that threatened to do to him what one had done to Nick.

Felucci turned and ran toward the house, impeded by his excessive weight. Just short of the back door he stopped, fell to his knees and sprawled on the brick walk. He struggled to rise, then jerked and fell on his face. Bolan glanced at Bonnie, who was grimly firing rounds into the obese, twitching body of the godfather of western Massachusetts.

A third hardman burst through the door of the building. He had some kind of automatic weapon and began to spray bursts wildly, anywhere. The rounds roared over Bolan's head, and he stopped them with a quick shot from the .44. The gunner was driven against the frame of the door by the force of the big slug, and he dropped the grease gun and toppled.

At the same time, another Mafia soldier ran from the house. Bonnie's second or third shot caught him in the belly, and he staggered back inside.

"Watch it!" Bolan yelled.

The van was hurtling toward them. The hardmen inside the vehicle had heard the gunfire and had returned.

Fortunately they had no idea where the attack on Felucci was coming from and though one of them hung out of the window of the vehicle with an Uzi ready to fire, he didn't know where to direct a burst. The Executioner snapped two shots into the grille of the van. The radiator exploded, but, more than that, the huge, high-velocity slug cracked the block, and the engine froze. Though the drive shaft broke, the van was thrown into a skid.

But the man beside the driver had seen Bolan's big fiery muzzle-flashes, and he loosed a burst toward the shadowy figures he could just make out on the ground outside the fence. Bullets shredded the wood, sending splinters cascading over Bolan and Bonnie.

"Down! Get down, you two!" Bolan shouted at the two handcuffed young people who were now trying to crawl toward the fence. "Fall on your bellies!"

The men from the van were EVA, and had a general idea where to direct their fire. Their bullets were coming close.

Bonnie emptied the Walther, firing wildly. Not one of the bullets found flesh, but the slugs kicking the ground and thunking into cars distracted the two hardmen and spoiled their aim.

The man who had crawled under the Mercedes was on his feet on the far side of the vehicle now—between the two sedans—and he, too, had an idea where his targets were. A shot from his revolver shattered a fence post just above Bonnie's position.

Bolan fired a shot through the windows of the Mercedes that sprayed glass on the gunman and stopped his fire for a moment. Then the warrior aimed a round at the car's gas tank, which missed. The second shot found its target, drilling a hole in the tank that leaked gasoline to the ground.

The .44 Desert Eagle was empty, the slide locked back, ready to take another clip. With quick, practiced motions, Bolan ejected the empty clip and shoved home a new one.

Bonnie, too, had reloaded. She fired two quick shots toward the driver of the van. He shrieked and danced back, behind the body of the van.

The guy behind the Mercedes recovered and fired again, barely missing Bonnie. His slug actually touched the heel of her shoe.

Bolan fired three quick shots at the gas tank, one generating a spark that caused an explosion.

The gunner behind the Mercedes raced into the open, beating his burning clothes with his hands in a frantic effort to put out the flames that were consuming him. He fell to the ground and rolled.

Bolan aimed at the van and sent a bullet through the windshield and into the body of the driver. The man howled in pain and terror. He had been hiding in there, clutching the small wound made by Bonnie's silenced killer, and now his shoulder was destroyed. Blood was gushing down his arm.

"No! No!" he screamed. "I surrender!"

One man was left, the one with the Uzi. He had run behind the concrete-block building, and now he shoved the subgun around the corner and fired a long burst. But it wasn't aimed, and it was too long. After a moment he threw the Uzi on the ground beyond the burning car and stepped out with his hands above his head. Bonnie leveled the PPK, and before Bolan could stop her, put a 7.65 mm slug in the gunner's chest.

6

The gagged and handcuffed girl rose to her knees and stared around, her wide eyes reflecting the roaring flames from the burning Mercedes. Her companion rolled toward her and scrambled up on his knees, glancing from one bloody corpse to the next. Felucci's farm had become a death ground. They stared toward the fence, toward the unseen people who had saved them. Bolan and Bonnie hadn't yet thought it safe to rise and cross the fence—there might be more gunmen in the house or in the concrete-block building.

Bolan finally stood, stepped over the shattered fence and walked toward the couple, followed by Bonnie. He untied the rope that held the gag in the young man's mouth, Bonnie doing the same for the young woman.

"What did *you* do to Felucci?" Bonnie asked as the girl spat out the rag that had almost choked her.

"Owed...money," she gasped. She was pretty—a plump young blonde, not more than twenty years old.

The young man was dark haired, emaciated, and had a bad complexion. "We owed him eight thousand," he said hoarsely. "With vigorish it was another hundred every day. Felucci wanted to turn her out on the street to earn it. Hell, she couldn't have made the vig."

Bolan went through the pockets of the driver, then of the other man from the van and found the key to the handcuffs. He released the girl first, then let her free the young man.

"You two are ...?"

"My name's Dick Greenberg, and she's my wife, Lynn."

"And you were into Felucci for which? Coke?"

Greenberg nodded. "Coke. Both of us. Me worse."

"Well, we'd better move," Bolan told them. "The police will be here any minute, and I'd rather not have to explain the bodies."

He looked around for Bonnie and spotted her kneeling over Felucci, going through his pockets. She pulled out the wad of cash, and before he could tell her to hurry, Greenberg quickly walked to the body of the driver and took the money Felucci had given him.

"Let's *go*, dammit!" Bolan snapped.

BY THE TIME they reached the rented Ford, parked two hundred yards up the road from the Felucci house, the first howling, flashing police car careered onto the grounds. Bolan drove away quietly into the darkness, without touching either the headlight switch or the brake pedal, which would have illuminated the car's rear lights.

"There's more to it, kids," he said to the Greenbergs as he concentrated on the darkened road. "Felucci didn't have you hauled out here to murder for eight thousand."

"Who are you?" Greenberg asked.

"We're the people who just saved your life half a minute short of having your heads blown off."

"Most of it's like Dick said," Lynn whispered. "Except for one little thing. We weren't into Felucci for coke we sniffed ourselves. We were dealing. He let us buy on a pay-later basis. We bought, we sold, we paid him. Then somebody ripped us off for about three thou worth. I mean, a guy with a gun took it away from us. And we couldn't pay Felucci.''

"Three thou," Greenberg said. "Up to eight in just a few months."

"The interest," Bolan concluded.

"Yeah. Vig on the three. Then vig on the vig. In a little while we'd have owed the guy a million."

"So," Lynn added, "we talked to the narcs."

"Suicide," Bonnie grunted.

"Yeah . . ." said Lynn bitterly. "One of them talked to Felucci. One of the bastards *betrayed* us. Damned narcs—"

"Both of you hooked?" Bolan asked.

"I am," Dick said.

"If I put you in touch with somebody who'd get you out of this whole deal, would you go?" Bolan asked. "Two conditions. You'd have to sit still for treatment, and you'd have to help somebody identify the narc who sold you out."

"One question," Greenberg said. "Who the hell are you?"

"Someone you'd be better off not knowing."

BOLAN AND HAL BROGNOLA had agreed to meet in the Chinese restaurant atop the Cambridge Hyatt Regency. Brognola, who appreciated good food, had ordered pressed duck and a young Chateauneuf du Pape, a red wine powerful enough to cope with the savory meat that would soon be served. Mack Bolan, who usually paid less attention than Brognola did to what he ate and drank, had ordered steak and a beer.

"All right," Brognola began. "Business. Debriefing the Greenbergs, we got a line on a corrupt narc." He shrugged. "So what else is new?"

Bolan lifted the glass containing the dregs of his beer. "Okay," he said. "Thank God for small favors and pass on to bigger issues."

"In a few days, you've blasted a big hole in Massachusetts. The boys are going to cover. Felucci . . . I'm not sure you know what you did. I—"

"Personal matter, I didn't like wasting time on it at first, but—"

"It got more important as it went along," Brognola interrupted. "I follow. And so do they. The New England Families know Bolan is back. You won't hit another one so easy. They're surrounding themselves with guns as well as other things—electronics. Felucci was the last of the old school. Don't think you can get Frenchi the same way."

"DiRosario's mole is back inside."

"A lot of guts, that girl." Brognola sighed. "I wouldn't give you a nickel for her chances."

"They taught her lessons, and she learned well. It was Bonnie who shot Felucci, not me."

Brognola glanced around the restaurant. They were high above the Charles River, and through the huge windows of the dining room they had a view of all of Boston. "I can't promise you we could have held him. The news people are mixed about him. Some say a big gangster was killed in a gang shoot-out. Others are saying an honest businessman has been the victim of a brutal murder." The big Fed shrugged. "Striker—"

"The old story," Bolan said, dismissing the subject. "I heard it first time around. Remember Mack Bolan, Public Enemy Number One?"

"All right," Brognola growled, "you've cut a big hole in the New England Mafia. But Ron Elliott's dead, and—"

"The hole doesn't lead us to his killers," Bolan finished.

Brognola nodded. "You've blasted some bad guys. The world is better off. But we're no closer to whoever wasted Ron."

"My idea was to work in one of the warehouses," Bolan said, "to find out who was doing the hijacking. Trouble is—I *know* who's doing it."

"How about taking a ride in an air freighter?" the big Fed suggested. "See how the thieves operate."

"IT WAS BUILT to carry about eighty passengers," Russ Caldwell, the pilot began. "At one time she could make three hundred miles per hour. Now the poor old girl carries about fifteen thousand pounds of cargo, and we're hard put to get two-seventy out of her. But I'll tell you, Major Morrison—she's a good old airplane with thousands of hours left in her. Dundee treats these old planes right. They get good service, so they give good service."

Caldwell spoke in a tone that was probably natural to him—loud enough to be heard over the throbbing roar of the four big radial engines that powered the old DC-6. The copilot had gone back for coffee, and Bolan sat in his seat.

They had taken off from Boston early in the morning. The flight was to Miami, where a cargo would be off-loaded and replaced with a northbound cargo, after which the DC-6 would head back for Boston. It was a day's work for pilots and airplane—about nine hours in the air and about four on the ground in Miami. It would be a longer day for Bolan, who had been at the airport three hours before the DC-6 was to take off so he could watch the loading, and he would stay around the Dundee hangar and warehouse until the airplane was unloaded.

Tom Dundee had introduced him to the flight crew as a federal inspector who would watch the loading and unloading as well as join them on the flight. He would be checking weight and balance as well as how the plane was flown, which explained why he paid so much attention to how the plane was loaded.

The two pilots had been told he was really Major MacKenzie Morrison, investigating Ron Elliott's death. Tom Dundee insisted the men were to be trusted. Caldwell especially was offended by the intrusion of criminals into a business he regarded as something more than a business. For him, flying was almost a mystic calling. He had done it all his life, first in the Air Force, then for an airline, now for an air-freight company. He was a bulky, red-haired man, dressed in a white shirt with the blue-gold shoulder tabs of an aircraft captain. His dark blue cap was on the shelf behind his seat. Though he was flying freight, he lived by the proprieties—as British barristers wear wigs and robes even when prosecuting or defending a pickpocket or pornographer.

"I'd rather fly freight," he admitted. "There's no obligation to stand in the door and smile at the cargo as it leaves the plane."

Aside from the two pilots, the crew of the DC-6 consisted of a supercargo and his assistant. They didn't move freight but were charged with seeing to it that the freight matched the documents and that the airplane carried what it was supposed to be carrying. Dundee thought they were honest, too, though he didn't vouch for them the way he did for the pilots.

Behind the cockpit was the head and a small cabin with four seats. It was equipped with a coffee maker and insulated hot and cold chests for food and drink. Behind the cabin the fuselage of the airplane was open for almost its full length, making a long, cigar-shaped cargo space. It was only about half-filled, with scores of wooden crates. Many more crates were being carried in the cargo hold beneath the floor, where passengers' luggage had been stowed in the days when the DC-6 was an airliner. All these crates were filled with desktop computers.

Shortly after takeoff from Boston, the DC-6 had climbed through the cloud cover into an open space between that layer and one about two thousand feet above it. They had flown in the clear for more than a thousand miles, with unlimited horizontal visibility and nothing but clouds in sight above and below. Then the clouds broke, first above, then below, and they flew the last hour in brilliant sunshine with green land and blue ocean beneath.

Bolan sat behind the pilots on the approach to landing, in what had been the flight engineer's seat in days gone by. Russ Caldwell had suggested he sit there. It served to confirm the story that he was a federal inspector.

The big old airplane required all the attention of the two pilots as they descended into the heavy traffic and set up an approach to Miami International. While they were busy reconfiguring the airplane's systems for lower and slower flight, the controllers added to their burden by constantly calling new courses and altitudes. They eased back their throttles and reduced engine speed, changed the pitch of the propellers, enriched the fuel-air mixture, lowered flaps, lowered the landing gear. The controller warned them of an unidentified light aircraft at the one o'clock position and closing, altitude unknown. The copilot had to scan the skies for him—finding him, ultimately, passing under the DC-6, two thousand feet below.

Their approach was set up on what pilots call a right base for Runway 27 Right, which meant they flew south until it was time to make a 90-degree turn to the right onto the runway heading. Big jets coming in on faster straight-in approaches for the same runway passed in front of them. Bolan watched the last of these, a Pan Am 747, roar across their course only a couple of miles ahead of the DC-6—as he judged the distance—and then Caldwell was cleared for final approach and banked the DC-6 slowly onto the runway heading. The 747 touched down while they were still about five miles out, and they were cleared to land.

Final approach seemed dull and slow. The touchdown point, just beyond the threshold of the runway, remained in the center of the windshield, looking bigger as the DC-6 came closer. They crossed over some houses, then a highway, and suddenly they were over the airport land. Caldwell hauled back on his yoke, the plane's nose rose so high that Bolan could no longer see the touchdown point and then the wheels were shrieking against the ground.

"ALL I KNOW for sure," Russ explained as he and Bolan stood inside the hull of the DC-6 and watched forklifts unload the cargo, "is that what was aboard when we taxied away from the Dundee hangar this morning was aboard when we taxied up to this hangar."

Bolan had followed the forklifts into the hangar. They went straight to a storage room, made from wood and chicken wire, where the crates of computers were counted and stacked. When the first storage room was filled, it was padlocked and another was opened.

The storage rooms were flimsy—the chicken wire was meant to identify areas more than to secure them—but they were under the eyes of several guard stations. To steal a crate, a thief would have to corrupt a guard.

"It's the same way we do it in Boston," Caldwell continued. "Storage areas… There are documents for all those boxes, and the boxes are numbered. Tomorrow or the next day some computer store in Florida will complain that it ordered fifty computers and only got forty-five."

"And flying back," Bolan said, "likely as not we'll be carrying a load of cocaine."

Caldwell nodded. "Sometimes they blame me. I've been investigated, interrogated and I've come close to being charged, I guess. After all, how could a pilot not know what he's carrying in an airplane?"

"What *are* we carrying back?"

"Look what's lining up," Caldwell replied.

He pointed to three big trucks that had pulled up to the rear of the airplane, waiting for the aircraft to be unloaded before moving closer with their load. The trucks were painted with a smiling tomato, the logo of XL-ENT Produce Company.

Tomatoes were the return cargo, as Bolan learned when the loading began—tomatoes, individually wrapped in tissue paper and packed in compartmented paper boxes, that would sell for three dollars and more a pound in New England markets. The square paper boxes were loaded into the airplane in wooden frames that prevented the weight of boxes above from pressing down on boxes below—eight boxes to a frame.

Federal and state inspectors examined the boxes as they were lifted out of the trucks and loaded into the DC-6—narcs, customs inspectors, agriculture inspectors. Some of them had dogs that walked around the boxes, sniffing. From time to time an inspector opened a box and lifted out a tomato. And the loading continued. They found nothing in the boxes but tomatoes.

Vans arrived bringing other cargo. The inspectors looked into six crates of camera lenses, twenty crates of magnetic disks and a dozen tall paperboard wardrobes filled with clothes on hangers. Then a hearse eased to a stop at the rear of the plane and a casket was loaded into the bottom cargo hold. Caldwell explained that the contents of the casket would have been examined at the funeral home, where it would have been sealed. It would be inspected again in Boston to ensure the seals were intact.

"I've watched this operation a thousand times," Caldwell stated. "We don't lose cargo in the air, for damn sure. We lose it in the warehouses on both ends. And the narcotics, well they get it by some how."

"Has any ever been found on a plane you were flying?" Bolan asked.

"Three trips back," Caldwell told him, "they found bags of coke in hollowed-out books. Supposed to be a collection of rare old books on its way to a Boston dealer. They were rare old books, too—all covered in cracked leather, dusty, yellowed—but they'd been opened and cut to make hidey-holes inside. A Colombian. One of the Florida narcs was so upset to see that those valuable old books had been destroyed that he damn near broke the Colombian's jaw. Anyway, that's not the only time. Some of the narcs know I don't have anything to do with it. Some of them don't."

Bolan smiled wryly. "You ever hear of coke being hidden in tomatoes?"

Caldwell nodded toward the men poking around the boxes of tomatoes. "No. But how could they check every tomato in every box? There's thousands of them. What's more, you'd destroy a lot of them, packing and unpacking." He shook his head. "As long as the stuff comes in, as long as people want to buy it, there's no way to stop its being sneaked into air shipments, rail shipments... whatever. Unless someone can find some way to make it so the risk's not worth the profits. And the profits are high. You have to—''

"Kill them?" Bolan asked.

"I've thought of it often. A guy like me can't do much. Maybe you can. Anyway, anything I can do to help—just mention it."

THE RETURN FLIGHT was uneventful. The landing at Logan was like the one at Miami International, only this one involved coming down through heavy cloud in the dark. One minute the night was black—no light at all except faint red reflections the plane's navigation lights made on the insides of clouds—the next minute the jewellike runway lights of Boston Logan were directly ahead and the DC-6 was within a mile of touchdown.

As an "inspector," Bolan stood on the ramp and watched the unloading of the big airplane. As before, federal and state agents poked into the cargo as it was transferred from the plane to the warehouse-hangar. Documents were checked, and as Caldwell said, what was loaded in Miami was unloaded in Boston.

But in the next few hours, part of the cargo would disappear.

Bolan made a show of saying goodbye to the two pilots and walking out through the Dundee hangar to catch a cab. He managed to hail a taxi and ordered the driver to take him to the main passenger terminal, where DiRosario and Lindsay were waiting for him in an office.

"Here's what you ordered, Chief," DiRosario said, handing Bolan a pair of Gunderson Night Vision Goggles.

They were a heavy device, yet comfortable enough to wear. The warrior fitted them over his eyes, adjusted the straps behind his head and switched them on. Lindsay turned off the lights in the office, but Bolan could see the two FBI agents and everything in the office as clearly as if the overhead fluorescents had still been on. Except for color, the scene was completely natural and well defined. If anything, it was a little too bright, and he adjusted the system to reduce brightness.

"Okay, turn on the lights," Bolan ordered, taking off the goggles. "Have you got my 93-R?"

Lindsay opened his briefcase and handed Bolan the Beretta. The silencer and flash suppressor were in place, and the magazines were loaded with subsonic cartridges.

"Let's get back over there," Bolan said. "I wouldn't want to miss the show."

A few minutes later Bolan was outside the Dundee hangar. Tom Dundee had left his office window unlocked and the alarm sensor disabled. The warrior entered quietly, checked his surroundings then slipped out of the office and into the cavernous expanse of the warehouse-hangar.

The unloading had been finished, and the huge hangar doors, which were moved in their tracks by powerful electric motors, had been closed. A uniformed guard sat just inside those doors, beside a small door that was set in one of the big ones. The gooseneck lamp on his desk was the only light burning in the building, other than the red-and-white Exit signs above the street doors.

One airplane—a high-wing, twin-engine Mitsubishi—sat in the middle of the floor, awaiting repairs to one of its engines. Freight stood in specially designated areas around the floor. The cartons of tomatoes had been stacked near the hangar doors, so they could be quickly loaded on trucks in the morning. Other freight rested on pallets that would be lifted by the forklifts onto freight trucks or other Dundee planes, heading for their final New England destinations.

With the Gunderson goggles, everything was as clearly visible to Bolan as if the hangar had been brightly lighted. He made a small adjustment to the goggles and walked farther out into the hangar, looking for a place where he could hide and observe.

He suspected the narcotics—if in fact there had been any on the flight from Miami—were in the tomatoes. The narcs suspected so, too, but as Caldwell had said, they couldn't go through every carton, perhaps damaging a good part of the cargo just to indulge a suspicion. They had checked randomly among the boxes, and their dogs had sniffed around. They had done their job and passed on to another hangar, where another plane and its cargo had to be examined.

Bolan found a hiding place—in the cockpit of the Mitsubishi, from where he had a view of the cargo of tomatoes and of a good part of the hangar. Because the Mitsubishi was a low-slung airplane, he wasn't elevated above the freight stacked around the warehouse, but he had a good view of what he wanted to see, close up and from excellent concealment.

He didn't have long to wait. After twenty minutes the guard got up from his desk, opened the small door and admitted four men. The guard went outside, closing the door after him.

The new arrivals knew what they were doing. One of them opened the gray steel panel that contained the door controls, and the big hangar doors slid silently back. A van pulled in and the doors slid shut.

The vehicle was white, with black stripes, and on the roof it carried a stroboscopic dome light that would flash amber when it was turned on. The van was marked with the name and seal of the airport authority and the men wore the uniforms of the airport security police.

As Bolan had expected, they were interested in the tomatoes. But not just any boxes of tomatoes—specifically marked boxes. They had flashlights, and they searched among the boxes looking, apparently, for a mark on a crate. They occasionally pulled one out and set it aside. In a few minutes they had pulled about forty boxes.

"Better check," Bolan heard one man say. "We show up with a load of goddamn tomatoes, our butts are in a sling."

One of them knelt beside a box, pulled a knife, slit the lid and extracted a tissue-wrapped tomato from the box. He pulled off the tissue, felt the skin of the ripe tomato and used the blade of his knife to pry out a plug. He then extracted a glass vial.

"Okay," he grunted. "Satisfied?"

The tomatoes had probably been injected with some chemical to harden them, then cored from the stem ends with sharp knives, and sealed glass vials had been inserted. That was why the dogs hadn't smelled the cocaine—the stuff was sealed inside glass. It was likely, too, that some chemical had been used to conceal whatever slight odor of cocaine might remain. The stem ends of the tomatoes had been reinserted, and a wax had been rubbed over the cuts to hide them and prevent juice from leaking.

Bolan guessed each box contained forty-eight tomatoes. If all the tomatoes in the forty or fifty cartons were stuffed with vials of cocaine, this shipment contained at least two thousand vials. A plague of cocaine.

The warrior backed out of the cockpit of the Mitsubishi and stepped out onto the hangar floor.

"Okay. Let's get 'em in the van and get out of here."

Bolan set the Beretta to fire a 3-shot burst, took aim on the stacked cartons of tomatoes and fired. The silenced slugs ripped through four or five cartons of tomatoes, shattering scores of glass vials of narcotics, mixing them with chemically tainted tomato juice.

The four wise guys froze. They saw the boxes jump under the impact and saw the juice wet the paperboard. They understood what was happening, understood it just in time to stand rigid, unable to interfere, when a second 3-shot burst tore through their valuable merchandise.

"Jeez!" one of them screamed.

He threw himself into the van through the open back door and scrambled for the driver's seat. The others followed him. Before the fourth man was inside, the driver had already started the engine and thrown the van in gear. The vehicle shot forward, then stopped as the driver realized the hangar doors were closed. He jumped out and threw the switch and as soon as the doors were open wide enough, he accelerated. The van shot through the opening and disappeared into the night.

Bolan walked across the hangar floor to one of the forklift trucks and started it. Slowly, methodically, he raised the fork and then brought it down on the crates containing the drugs. The descending fork worked like a juice squeezer. Carton after carton collapsed under the pressure, with the tomatoes bursting and the vials of cocaine shattering. Within a few minutes a red stain was spreading across the floor of the hangar—with a dusting of white powder floating on top.

7

Ron Elliott had believed in what he did. He had known it could cost him his life, and he'd warned his wife, Janice, about that, even before they were married. During their years together they had lived with that threat hanging over them. And there had been separations. He'd never been at home. It was always something: a brushfire war here, terrorists there, drug dealers somewhere else...something vitally important to the lives of other people.

That was the whole thing—Ron Elliott had devoted his life to saving the lives of others. Sometimes they had argued about it, she saying he owed more to his family, if not to himself, he insisting his work was so important he couldn't stop to think what it cost himself and his family.

So here she was, forty-three years old, a widow...And what? What life was left for her? Fortunately she had something better to do than sit around watching television, grieving. The kids—Ron, Jr. and Brenda—had their lives organized, both in college, both sure of what they wanted to do in life. Brenda was at home one more day. Ron, Jr. had gone back to Princeton after his father's funeral. Janice was already getting calls—where was she, when would she be able to get back to work? She was an artist. In her husband's long absences she had learned to paint and to sculpt, and had gained some celebrity on the local art scene. She sold her works through surrounding galleries and even had a dealer in Washington.

Janice had loved Ron Elliott. There had never been any question about that, and during his absences she had been faithful to him, confident he was being faithful to her. Even so, within a few days of his death she couldn't help but wonder whether there was another man for her, a man to last the rest of her life.

She was an attractive woman. Her face was so regular in shape that she thought of it as unmemorable—greenish blue eyes under well-defined but not thick brows, high cheekbones concealed under a little too much flesh, a wide, expressive mouth, loose dark brown hair—and her figure was generous.

Janice and Brenda were sitting at the dinner table in the suburban home Ron had always insisted he loved but where he had spent so little time.

"It doesn't count for much to know he was a hero, does it?" Brenda asked.

Janice looked up from her plate. She understood it was something Brenda had been holding back for a long time, so she made no challenging remark; she just shook her head.

"When I think of the slime he—"

"That's the point," her mother interrupted. "His life's work was to exterminate the slime. And he did. He was good at it. More than you or I will ever guess, Brenda. And he knew—"

"I didn't mean to suggest I didn't respect him. Or what he did."

"We don't really know what he had to deal with. Oh, we think we do. But we don't. We live in a community that—" She stopped and forced back the sob that had crept into her throat. "We live in a community that exists

because of what your father did. None of us could
live—"

"Mom—"

"You understand. A little, anyway."

Janice poured the last of a bottle of Beaujolais into her
own glass, stared into it a moment, then drank.

"Mom, somebody's at the door."

THE KIDNAPPING was carried out quickly and efficiently.
Before Janice knew it, she lay doubled up in the trunk of
a car, her hands cuffed behind her back. Her mouth was
stuffed with a rag, and a piece of rope burned her lips,
preventing her from spitting the rag out. Brenda was...
Well, she could only hope Brenda was in the trunk of another car. She had seen them cuffing and gagging her. At
least she was alive.

They were making a long trip, though she had no idea
how much time had passed or where they were going. She
did guess, from the way the car sped along a road and
never stopped, that they were on an interstate highway,
heading... God knew where.

"THEY'RE NOT KIDDING," Brognola growled.

Mack Bolan stared at the Polaroid pictures the big Fed
handed him of Janice Elliott and her daughter Brenda,
holding up copies of yesterday's *Boston Globe*.

The message accompanying the two Polaroids, boldly
printed with a felt tip pen, was succinct: "Tell Bolan to lay
off. We're no suckers anymore. He lays off—or else."

"I guess we know what the 'or else' is."

"I guess we do," Bolan agreed.

"We've got to attack, keep the pressure on. It's the only
way to deal with a hostage situation."

"There's only one way to deal with hostage takers," Bolan agreed, "and that's to make it hurt. You make them hurt so bad they beg you to take your hostages back."

"I talked to the Man," Brognola said. "The word is go ahead. Cesare Frenchi is defying the law, defying decency."

"I'm going to free Janice Elliott, too, while I'm at it. I want you to call your FBI guys back. Lindsay and DiRosario are upright men—too upright for how I'm going to handle Frenchi. What I need is soldiers."

"Stony Man troops?" asked Brognola.

"No. I want two people—Bonnie Hennings and Umberto Lugano."

"Bonnie . . . ?"

"She's got a fire in her gut," Bolan explained. "She hates Frenchi. She has her reasons. What's more, she knows her way around."

Brognola shrugged. "You so rarely ask for a hand that you're entitled to pick your help. But, uh, Lugano? Really?"

"Lugano," Bolan repeated firmly.

UMBERTO "BIG LUG" LUGANO shuffled into an ugly, Spartan office in the administration building of Atlanta Federal Penitentiary. He shuffled because his ankles were linked by the short chain of his shackles. A security chain circled his waist, and the handcuffs locked on his wrists were attached to that chain, not together in front, but separately on each hip. He was dressed in blue jeans and a blue denim jacket.

"Unhook him," Bolan ordered.

The two uniformed guards frowned, and one asked, "You sure?"

"I'm sure. Unhook him, then leave us alone."

"You've got a lot of authority, mister—whoever you are," the guard said. "I don't think you've got too many brains."

"He don't," Lugano grunted as one guard knelt to unlock his leg irons and the other unlocked his handcuffs.

The guards left the room and closed the door, leaving Bolan sitting in a battered wooden chair behind a little wooden desk, staring at the big man just released from his chains.

"Why don't I just kill you?" Lugano asked.

"Why don't you try? It didn't work out when you tried before, but maybe you've got stronger and smarter since you've been in stir."

"Yeah," Lug Lugano muttered. "Not likely, huh?"

"How would you like a presidential pardon?"

"How would you like to go to hell?"

Bolan grinned. "You can be more kinds of damned fool than any man I ever saw."

Lug Lugano sighed. "So you said once before. And I'd have to be another kind of fool to think the President is going to pardon Umberto Lugano. I wasted a Sugar, and I've been a bad boy every day I've been here."

"Your shooting the Fed surprised me," Bolan said shortly. "Your being a bad boy here doesn't."

"You know how it happened."

"You have a foul temper, Lug."

"Well, thank you, Chaplain Bolan. Or are you playing shrink?"

Bolan leaned back and assessed the man, as he had done many times before.

Umberto Lugano bore the scars of being known since childhood as the toughest guy on the block, wherever he was, including here in the federal penitentiary. When Bolan first saw him in Vietnam, Lug's face had already been marked with thin knife scars and a shattered nose, which he'd gotten on the streets of Cleveland.

He'd been a tough, bold soldier, able to carry more weight for longer than other men, until they dropped from exhaustion and he was still pressing forward—capable, too, of killing without hesitation. But he never got a stripe—not even PFC—and nothing good on his record, only that he'd punched out a corporal, threatened a lieutenant with a knife, drank a Saigon bar dry then burned it to the ground.

Most officers were afraid of him. Rather than lock Lugano up, they sent him to do dirty work. If he didn't get himself killed—and most of them wouldn't have cared if he had—he could crawl in the muck, find the booby traps, draw sniper fire . . . make himself useful.

Big Lug didn't get himself killed. He served his hitch, and the Army grudgingly granted him an honorable discharge. He went back to Cleveland and picked up where he'd left off. Only by then he wasn't just a tough kid anymore; he was a tough man, who soon built a name as a guy you didn't cross unless you were willing to make big trouble for yourself.

But mostly he made big trouble for himself.

Bolan had encountered Lugano during the war against the Napolitano Family. The Napolitanos had understood how to handle someone like Umberto Lugano, and he had been a trusted, valued man. They had also known how to use him.

He'd been in the penitentiary for eight years. Long enough, Bolan thought. It was time to let Big Lug redeem himself—if he could.

"How would you like to go to war again, Lug? Maybe get yourself killed?"

Lug turned down the corners of his mouth and glanced around the place where they sat. "Might as well," he grunted.

"You remember Ron Elliott?"

Lug frowned. "Yeah. Yeah, I remember him. Sergeant Elliott. Decent guy. Different from most of— Well, you know what I mean. My Army time might have been different if there'd been more sergeants like Ron Elliott."

Bolan nodded. "Ron's dead. Wasted last week by some wise guys in Boston. Worse yet, they've kidnapped his wife and daughter."

"Why, for God's sake?"

Bolan sighed. "He stayed in the Army, made a career. Moved into Army intelligence, became an officer, retired a colonel. Then he went to work for the Feds. He was working undercover in Boston, trying to break up a hijacking operation, when they murdered him. Shot him in the knees, then in the head."

"And you're making war on the guys that did it."

"You better believe it."

Big Lug blew out a noisy breath, then shrugged. "Well . . . why you talking about a pardon?"

"You know your way around," Bolan said. "You know some of the guys involved, know how they work, how they think—"

"I been eight years out of circulation."

"You remember Guido Terranova?"

Lug nodded. "An animal."

"He's Cesare Frenchi's enforcer. Probably the man who shot Ron in the knees, which is his style."

"Frenchi," Lug mused. "That little punk. I heard he's revived the Frenchi Family. Strictly off the reservation."

"Well, maybe the Commission doesn't think so. He's got his territory, in Boston, and his button men and soldiers. They kidnapped Janice Elliott and her daughter to hold as hostages. They sent word that if I don't lay off, they'll kill both mother and daughter."

"You want *me* to go gunning against these guys? Why me? I hear you've got contacts, and backup if you need it."

"If I remember right," Bolan replied, "you've got guts, and you know the kind of men we'll be up against. You're not stupid—though you've gone to a lot of trouble to prove you are, for years. I don't know what this place has done to you, probably nothing good. But maybe you've learned to hold your temper, at least a little. Also, I figured you'd be willing to do something for Ron."

"You're talking about getting me out of here."

Bolan nodded. "In my custody. And if you do a good job for me, rumor has it you might get a full pardon."

Umberto Lugano clasped his hands, cracking his knuckles. "I remember when the Feds wanted you more than they did me."

"They've learned to appreciate me," Bolan said dryly.

"You want to trust me?"

"I figure I can take a chance on you."

Big Lug leaned back in his chair and regarded Bolan with an intent, skeptical stare. "Well, maybe I can take a chance on you, too." He shrugged. "Hell, what've I got to lose?"

THEIR DISORIENTATION was complete. Neither woman had any idea where they were. They had talked about it, compared what they had heard, but they couldn't make sense of it. The women had been flown somewhere. Blindfolded, gagged and with their hands cuffed behind them, they had been taken somewhere in a car, then somewhere in an airplane. They were far from home; there was no question about that. But where?

The basement room where they were confined had no windows. Two bare mattresses on the floor served as their beds. The usual purpose of the room was evident enough. It was furnished with a Ping-Pong table, as well as three cheap vinyl-upholstered armchairs, one of them a recliner. The room was paneled in knotty pine, which was scarred and nicked. A small stone fireplace was stained with smoke and tar.

Janice and Brenda had pulled two of the vinyl-covered chairs together. They had to, if they wanted to sit in them, because about three feet of chain fastened with two padlocks joined Janice's right ankle to Brenda's left.

Brenda had come to dinner the night before last in a white dress that left her tanned shoulders bare. She was still wearing it. She and her mother were barefoot—their captors had taken their shoes. Her makeup was gone, and her face was a little bland and ill defined, and swollen from crying. She was nineteen years old, a pretty blonde with hair down to her shoulders, and like her mother, a little heavy, a little soft.

They saw little of the men who held them prisoner. One came into the basement three times a day with food. He brought them wine, too, and even a quart of Scotch. Be comfortable, he'd said.

Which, of course, was impossible. They could only guess why they had been kidnapped and what was going to happen to them. And when. They could only worry and wonder.

"THEY WENT CRAZY! When they heard about Felucci, they went absolutely crazy. If Cesare had any idea I had anything to do with it..." Bonnie shuddered.

Any man who had ever been issued one would have recognized Lugano's dark blue suit as the sturdy, unstylish suit handed to a convict on release. He had bought new clothes that were in the process of being altered. A bulky, rugged man, Lugano kept his hair clipped short, maybe to hide the fact it was turning gray along the sides. When he was dressed in a suit, white shirt and necktie, his battered nose and knife scars were more evident than they had been when he wore his prison denims. He sucked on the butt of a cigarette, which he held tightly between his thumb and first two fingers.

"You don't have to do this," Bolan said to Bonnie.

"The hell I don't. If Cesare Frenchi hasn't figured it out yet, he will. You can't walk out on a man like him. He's got a memory like Felucci had."

"So we'll fix him the same way," Lug said.

"Maybe," Bolan replied. "The job is to break up the racket, plug one of the holes where narcotics come into this country, stop the leak of merchandise. Also, the job is to save the lives of Janice and Brenda Elliott. If Cesare Frenchi happens to get hurt in the process..." He shrugged. "But it's not the priority."

"DiRosario wasn't happy," Bonnie said. "He was real fond of having a mole inside Frenchi's house. But like I said, they went crazy when they found out about Felucci. I mean, the Frenchis have locked the doors shut and pulled in the sidewalks. If I'd stayed, I couldn't have gotten out for any more meets with DiRosario."

"But if you—"

She interrupted. "Right. I don't *have* to do anything. I can sit around someplace and wait to see if you guys can solve my problem. Let me explain it this way, Mack. If you waste Cesare Frenchi, then maybe I got some kind of life ahead of me. If you don't, I don't—for sure. You understand that, you understand why you can count me in."

"We can put you in the federal witness protection program," Bolan suggested.

"Oh, sure," she sneered. "I can go live in Cincinnati. Count me in, Mack."

Bolan nodded. "All right. So, now we've got to do some planning. First thing I'd like to find out is where they're holding the Elliotts."

"They grabbed them in Baltimore, you say?" Big Lug asked.

"Actually a town a little closer to Washington."

"But not Washington. Not *in* Washington?"

"No. Maryland."

"Yeah, well, that's Sestola's territory. And I don't figure Frenchi would grab those two women out of Sestola's territory without Sestola's okay. So, let's go after Sestola."

"It's the only key we've got," Bolan concurred.

"We—"

Big Lug was interrupted by a knock on the door. They were meeting in a room in a West Roxbury motel. Lug and Bonnie drew pistols as Bolan went to the door.

It was Robert DiRosario.

"I'm sorry to bring you what I have to bring you," he said to Bolan as he opened his briefcase and took out a small box. Lying in the box, in a nest of white cotton, was a woman or girl's left-hand ring finger. He unfolded the message that had been enclosed:

"One off. Nine to go."

8

Vincenza Sestola was a contented man. He was sixty-four years old, and at his age the capo figured he was entitled to his contentment. His health was good, he had eighteen grandchildren and he was secure. All the old troubles were in his past—the fight to make his place in the world, the wars, the contest for his seat on the Commission, the little revolts of young guys who hadn't learned patience, troubles with the Feds... hell, a thousand things he'd had to worry about all his life. All that was past. The Commission had fixed territories and established peace among the Families. The administration in Washington was so busy chasing its tail that it pretty much left businessmen alone. All the young guys were in their place, which was firmly under his thumb. He was living the good life.

A part of the good life was being able to live a routine. He'd never figured that when he was younger, but it was true—it was great to be able to follow a regular routine. He left home about ten, after a leisurely breakfast with his wife of forty-four years, was driven to the Syracuse Sport Club, and until evening sat at his table, smoking cigars, chatting with friends, sipping wine, eating and doing business.

People who wanted to do business came to him. Once they had come to his office. Now they came here. Even this one, who sat across the table from him, came to the Syracuse Sport Club.

They spoke Italian.

"It's good, eh, Umberto? The pasta. It's good. You like it, eh?"

Umberto Lugano shoved another forkful of the linguine into his mouth and added a sip of red wine. He nodded. The Sicilian's pride in his food and wine was no surprise. They all had it, the old ones.

"You didn't get anything like that in Atlanta, I bet."

Lug shook his head. "Nothing like this, Don Vincenza. For eight years."

"And the wine," Sestola said. "Nothing like that. Imported from Sicily. Hmm? The good life, eh, Umberto?"

Lug nodded again, because his mouth was too full of food for him to answer.

He did appreciate the food and wine. He had missed it. He'd missed something else, too—a sense of danger, of risk, of confrontation. Sestola looked placid enough, reasonable enough, but Lug knew him for a snake at best, a mad dog at worst. That was what had made him what he was—dangerous.

It was hard to think so, looking at this man in his sixties: his bald head was liver spotted and tan, his hair was gray, he was loosely fat and had a heavy paunch. Sestola only nibbled at his pasta, probably because he'd already eaten a large portion or two earlier. He sipped his wine and rolled an unlighted cigar in his hands.

Though the cigar remained unlighted, it was evident that he did smoke, as witnessed by the accumulation of soft gray ash in the big Cinzano ashtray and by the ash stains on the white tablecloth.

"Pete! More wine," Sestola said to one of the men sitting at a nearby table.

They were his bodyguards, and had frisked Lug when he arrived—though Sestola had apologized for it, saying he was sure Umberto would understand why he was cautious. The bodyguards were armed. Unless Lug guessed wrong—and he rarely did about things like this—some very heavy weapons were handy behind the bar. Maybe a *lupara*, a big Sicilian shotgun loaded with the heavy shot that traditionally had been used to kill wolves. Maybe something more modern, such as an Uzi.

"Umberto," Sestola said, "tell me how you got out of the penitentiary."

Lug pushed another forkful of linguine into his mouth. "I'm sure you know."

"You work for Uncle Sugar, eh?" Sestola suggested scornfully. "To get out of prison, you—"

"I may be able to do you a service, Don Vincenza." Lugano was calm in the face of Sestola's sudden flush and scowl. "I hope so."

"And what of the code?" Sestola demanded, referring to *omertà*, the traditional code of silence that bound every made man. "What of that?"

"I've told them nothing. They've asked nothing. That's not what they want of me."

"Then what? Why have they sent you to me?"

"There was a sitdown," Lug said. "When was it? Last week? Between you and Cesare Frenchi."

"Why do you think that?"

"Frenchi is a mad dog, but he's not so mad as to come down to Maryland and kidnap two women without at least notifying you in advance about what he was going to do and why. But I suspect he lied to you, Don Vincenza. And he made trouble for you."

"What are you telling me, Umberto? What trouble?"

"Do you know who the two women are?" Lug asked.

Sestola shrugged. "Two women who caused him trouble, he said. He said he wanted to snatch them, to straighten out some business. He gave me their names, told me where they live. They meant nothing to me."

"They mean a great deal to you, Don Vincenza," Lug told him solemnly. "They are the wife and daughter of a Fed. The first thing Frenchi did was execute the man— knees and head. Now he's snatched the wife and daughter. What's more, he cut a finger off one of them and sent it to the FBI office in Boston."

"What's he trying to do, make war?"

"Worse than that," Lug replied. "He's got Bolan on the rampage again."

"*Bolan?* What's Bolan got to do with it?"

Lugano raised his glass of wine, stared into it for a moment, then took a sip. "The Sugar wasted by Frenchi was an old friend of Bolan's. For years the Executioner has been off our backs, doing other things mostly. By doing a knees-and-head on his old buddy, Frenchi brought him back. You know, we had to look for trouble if somebody wasted a Sugar. But *this* kind of trouble?"

Sestola frowned. "What's the idea of cutting off a woman's finger?"

"The idea of snatching the wife and daughter was to scare Bolan off. The wife and daughter are also friends of his, and Frenchi thinks he can use them as hostages and force Bolan to back away. He sent the finger to— Well, you know. Frenchi looks like he's been taking lessons from some of the crazies Bolan's been fighting the past few years."

Sestola sighed heavily and reached for the wine bottle. He poured himself a glass and drank a swallow. "I don't need this, Umberto. Nobody needs this. *Bolan*, for Chrissake! Bolan! Talk about a crazy man ... Anyway, what's he got against me? All I did was—''

"Authorize the snatch."

"I didn't know who they were, or why—"

"Not going to change Bolan's mind, Don Vincenza"

Sestola glanced toward his bodyguards. "Bolan's going to make war on me?" he asked quietly, so they wouldn't hear. "And what are you, his messenger boy?"

Lugano shrugged. "Call me that, if you want."

"What's the message?"

"Bolan wants to know where Frenchi's got the two women."

"Umberto, if I knew... I don't know if I'd tell you. But I don't know. Do I talk to you anymore about the honor of friends? I don't know. Are you a friend? Suppose you still are. On my word as a friend of the friends, I don't know. What's more, I didn't know who these women were when Frenchi came here and asked if it was okay to snatch them."

Lug sipped his wine. "I believe you, Don Vincenza. I'll tell Bolan I believe you."

Sestola shook his head. "A crazy man, that Bolan. And he got you out of the penitentiary, hmm? He trusts you? Tell him I don't need trouble with him. Another crazy man is Cesare Frenchi. A crazy man!"

"Bolan didn't think you'd know where the women are," Lug said. "He wants something else from you."

"What is that, Umberto?"

"He wants you to call Frenchi and tell him to send the women back."

"Oh, sure. Sure. I'll tell him that. Then he'll send *me* a finger."

"And he wants you to talk to the Commission."

Vincenza Sestola leaned back in his chair and for a long moment regarded Umberto Lugano with cold, calculating eyes. Then he nodded. "What Frenchi's done is stupid."

"Yes. A thing like this can put the Sugars in a mood to crusade. You know how they are—first one thing, then something else, whatever gets them the most publicity. Well, when the story of this snatch, plus the finger, hits the news . . . Don Vincenza, what could it cost having the Sugars on crusade? Even if it only lasts a couple of months?"

The thought made Sestola turn down the corners of his mouth and shake his head.

"I'll tell you what it could cost," Lug continued. "Half of what it cost to have Mack Bolan at war."

"All right, Umberto. You tell Bolan I'll pass the word."

"Good. And thank you, Don Vincenza. Thanks for an excellent meal. I don't remember when I've had as good. I know I've never had better."

"A word for you, Umberto," Sestola warned. "This thing you are doing—working with Bolan. You know you could get a serious headache."

Lug knew what that meant—that he could get a bullet in his head. "I told you I was doing you a service by bringing you this word. It's a service to the Commission, too. A service to all the Families. Let them understand that."

THE SITDOWN TOOK PLACE that same evening. The word that Bolan had returned to the old war was enough to bring the Commission together on short notice. Of course, not everyone was there. In fact, only four members made it. But others had called and given word that whatever the four decided would bind all the Families, at least until a full conference could be held.

They met in New York, in the Manhattan office of Giuseppe Rossi. Sestola flew up from Baltimore. Bill O'Neill drove down from Boston. The Philadelphia Families were represented by Albert Ferraro.

Rossi welcomed them into a handsome conference room on the forty-second floor of an office building owned by the real estate conglomerate his Family controlled. He looked like one of the distinguished businessmen that used to appear in whiskey ads—perfectly brushed white hair, a tanned, square face, a tailored gray suit with a vest. He deserved the name most of them knew him by—"Clean Joe."

"We'll miss Al Felucci," he said, opening the meeting.

"Whacked by Bolan," O'Neill added.

O'Neill looked like what he was—an Irishman, only a timid, conservative Irish schoolteacher. His face was pink, his eyes pale blue. He wore rimless eyeglasses, and his gray suit was styled like Rossi's but had probably cost a fifth as much.

"That's the point," Rossi said. "He's hit the Frenchi Family hard. Killed Al Felucci. And he's threatening—Well, tell us, Vincenza. What's he threatening?"

"The old war. And he's a crazy man."

"We have two choices," Ferraro observed. "One is to try to make the peace he suggests, by getting Cesare to release the Elliott women. The other is to make war in return." He shrugged. "I suppose there is a third choice—to do both."

Albert Ferraro had been an enforcer when he was a young man. He still looked dangerous. Although he was in his late fifties, Ferraro kept his hair jet black. He had a knife-sharp face, hard little eyes and wore his clothes with a flair that mocked the discreet business suits of the others.

"Peace with Mack Bolan," Sestola replied, "will be peace only as long as that's what he wants. The guy's a nut."

"Not a nut," Rossi corrected quietly. "A fanatic maybe, but not a nut. He's survived a dozen contracts, some of them for a lot of money. More than that, he's fought whole nations. Every kind of terrorist. I only wish there were some way to turn him. I don't think we've got much chance of giving him a big headache."

"Why does he come back to haunt us?" O'Neill asked. "I thought we'd—"

"A matter of priorities," Sestola broke in. "Bolan can't fight every war, not simultaneously. So he does what he can. When Cesare Frenchi killed the Fed at Boston Logan Airport, he accidentally killed a friend of Bolan's. And now, by snatching the Elliott women, he's *really* brought him down on our heads."

"So what do we do about it?" O'Neill asked.

"It's really very simple," Rossi replied smoothly. "You go back to Boston, Bill, and tell Cesare Frenchi the Commission orders him to release those two women immediately. That's my suggestion, and I so move."

"It's not going to get Bolan off our backs," Sestola warned. "He's going to want Frenchi's ass."

Rossi smiled sparely. "So? Maybe when he gets it, he'll be satisfied."

The following day a courier arrived at the offices of Rossi Enterprises, with a small box for Giuseppe Rossi, which he opened. Inside was a woman's finger—fifth finger, right hand. Clean Joe retreated to his bathroom and vomited.

SPECIAL AGENT DiROSARIO sat on the bed in the West Roxbury motel where Bolan had set up temporary headquarters with Lug Lugano and Bonnie Hennings. The FBI man was pale, and his forehead glistened with sweat. He kept shaking his head. He was, Bolan judged, on the verge of tears.

"'I didn't bring it," he said. "I didn't see any reason for you to have a look at it."

He had just told Bolan another package had arrived, containing an index finger, right hand.

"Not even any message," he continued. "I'll be altogether frank with you, Bolan. I don't know what to do."

"*We* know what to do," Lug countered.

He had put in a call to Sestola a little after noon, just checking with him to see whether any action had been taken, and had heard about the finger Rossi had received. He held in his right hand the .357 Magnum Colt Python revolver Bolan had issued him, and with his left hand he was spinning the cylinder. It was a nervous gesture, one of anger and frustration.

"I'm beginning to feel the way Lug does," Bolan growled. "I'm going to hit Frenchi where it hurts."

DiRosario shook his head. "Murdering, I can understand. I mean, I sort of can. But mutilating that woman and her daughter... I just don't know. I feel like breaking the rules. I feel like going in with you guys, to hell with the rules."

"No way," Bolan replied. "We need guys who play by the rules. That's your commitment, Bob. You stick to it."

"Sometimes—"

"Right," Bolan interrupted. "Sometimes it seems like it gets you nowhere. And that's when you're tempted to break the rules. But don't."

"But you—"

"Uh-uh. I don't break the rules. I just play by a different set. And that's *my* commitment."

DiRosario left. Bonnie had joined Lug in nervously toying with her weapon—a Beretta 93-R Bolan had issued to her as she joined his little team in the West Roxbury motel.

"Tactics," Bolan asserted. "We hit Frenchi where it hurts. We've got two choices, maybe. One is to go after him at his house. Literally hit him where he lives. The other is to hit him where he makes his money. I've done that already. Maybe the best chance of saving Janice and Brenda is to go after him directly. What do you think, Bonnie? Is he still there?"

"He was when I checked out. With armed guards all over the place."

"I need a sketch of the floor plan of the house," Bolan told her. "As much as you can remember. Every detail."

She nodded. "You got it."

"What happens if the cops come while we're moving in?" Lug asked. "You gotta figure Frenchi has some of them on the pad."

"Well, we can't shoot back at them, that's for sure. Even cops he's got on the pad. We have to move in and out, fast."

"I didn't sign up to commit suicide, Bolan."

"Neither did I, and neither did Bonnie. But you survived jobs where guys didn't care if you got killed or not. The difference here is, I *do* care."

Bonnie had pulled a big pad of ruled yellow paper from Bolan's kit and was already at work drawing the floor plan of the Frenchi house. "Me, too," she said. "I wouldn't want you to commit suicide, Umberto."

Bolan frowned for a quick moment, glancing back and forth between his two companions. He dismissed the idea that had come to his mind. He'd have time to think about that later.

He wondered for a moment whether it might not be better to call some of the men he knew he could depend on—men he could depend on *absolutely*, not just for their courage—because he didn't doubt the commitment of this pair—but for their professional experience, their cool determination in the face of odds. He decided not to call for them. Each of the Stony Man teams had vital work in hand. To call them off for this would be a poor use of resources. For this job he would depend on these two flawed recruits. He'd worked with worse people.

"We have our advantages," he said. "Not surprise. They'll be expecting us. What they don't know is that Bonnie is with us, which means they won't know we have a floor plan of the house. And we'll have some weapons that'll surprise them. Three people aren't going in after a dozen or twenty with nothing but side arms. You two are going to have to spend the next several hours learning how some things work."

"I oughta have confidence in you, you—" Lug started to say, but was interrupted by the telephone.

Hal Brognola was on the line, calling from Washington.

Without preamble the big Fed said, "Do you figure Cesare Frenchi is insane?"

"I don't know," Bolan replied. "Acts like it, doesn't he?"

"Well, let me give you some information you'll have to assimilate and judge the best you can. Sit down for this one, big guy.

"Okay. That severed finger; the grisly little present from Cesare Frenchi. Good news. It wasn't cut off Janice or Brenda Elliott. Fingerprints don't match. We have good prints for both of them, taken when Ron joined the group. You know, SOP. Do a background check, not just on your recruit, but on everybody associated intimately with him. It's not one of theirs. Not Janice's or Brenda's. No question.''

"Well, we've got two more.''

"I know about one," Brognola said. "The Boston FBI office sent the description—''

"One was also sent to the headquarters of the Commission, in New York. Frenchi's answer to their orders to let the two women go.''

Bolan waited out a long silence on Brognola's end of the telephone connection.

"Okay. Anyway, the one sent to the FBI office isn't from Ron's wife or daughter.''

"Then who *are* they from, Hal?" Bolan asked.

"More good news. The pathologist report on the one finger we've got in the lab says it was cut off a corpse. The thing had embalming fluid in it!''

Bolan was silent for a moment. "He had to know we'd figure that out in a little while.''

"He's playing games, Striker," Brognola affirmed. "If we've got good news in that he hasn't mutilated Janice or Brenda, we've got bad news in that he's for sure a mental case.''

"No idea where he's holding them?''

"No. We raided a couple of known places this afternoon. *Nada.* I don't know how you're going to get Ron's family back, except by getting your hands on that savage and cutting on him.''

"That's exactly what I've got in mind," Bolan replied grimly.

9

It was after midnight when Bolan and his team arrived on the quiet street where Cesare Frenchi lived. The mobster's house was a modest two-story red-brick structure on a narrow tree-lined street. A hundred and fifty years old, it had been remodeled along simple lines, so as not to attract attention. The pinkish old bricks had been cleaned, green shutters had been put on the windows, and the trim had been painted white.

The house had a cellar, which could be reached only by going down a flight of stone steps within the walled-in rear yard. The attic could be accessed only by pulling down a ladder in the ceiling of the second floor of the house. Bonnie had said the cellar and attic weren't used, except perhaps for storage.

One big bedroom upstairs had been turned into a kind of dormitory for the hardmen who remained around the house day and night. A smaller bedroom on the back of the house had been shared by Bonnie and a Sicilian girl named Clara. A third bedroom was a small guest room, often occupied by Salvatore Balestrino or Guido Terranova. The master bedroom, with its oversized master bath, belonged, of course, to Cesare Frenchi.

Bonnie tried to describe the security arrangements that protected the house. She admitted she knew very little about them, except that they were in place. The glass in all the windows was bulletproof, and the steel doors were secured by heavy locks. The building was protected by an electronic alarm system, but she had never discovered just how it worked.

The first floor was built on a center-hall plan, with a big living room to the right and a big dining room to the left. A library-study that Frenchi used for an office had been diminished by the installation of an odd-shaped bathroom on the rear of the house. There was a kitchen and a pantry and only one set of stairs led to the second floor.

She thought there would be at least five men in the house. But since Frenchi was expecting an attack, there was apt to be more. All would be heavily armed. What was more, there might be nasty surprises in the house—traps.

"Maybe we can arrange a nasty surprise or two of our own," was Bolan's comment.

The warrior was prepared for this fight, with some of his preferred weapons on hand. Because he didn't want to rouse the whole neighborhood, he had chosen sound-suppressed weapons for all of them. Each wore a Beretta 93-R in a quick-draw holster. He and Lug carried Heckler & Koch MP-5 SD submachine guns, which, like the Berettas, were equipped with flash suppressors and subsonic rounds. They had slung the H&Ks over their shoulders on straps, which enabled them to use their hands for other things. Bolan had hung four MU-50 grenades on his web belt. The lethal eggs were loaded with sharp bits of shrapnel that could rip through the bodies in a room without tearing out the walls.

And each member of the team had a pair of Gunderson goggles.

Bolan had driven past the house once before sunset and had an idea of how they would enter.

"The first thing I want to do is kill their telephones," he said to Lug. "Some alarm systems ring into a security-service office, and some ring right into police headquarters."

Lug nodded. "Some of them send the alarm signal when the telephone line is cut."

"Right. So what do you know about phone lines, Lug?"

"Not a damn thing. You pick up the phone, you get a dial tone. If you don't, you go next door and call for service."

"Okay. I want you and Bonnie to lie low—I mean *low*, both of you—while I do some work on the pole."

"We'll be in sight," Bonnie told him. "If anybody—"

"No. If a cop or a neighbor spots me and wants to know what I'm doing on the pole, you can't shoot."

They followed him into the alley behind the house to a utility pole that carried the telephone and power lines for several homes. Bolan waited for a minute or so, listening for signs that someone in the neighborhood had noticed three black-clad strangers in their alley. Nothing.

He climbed the pole.

The telephone job was a guess at best. Bolan pried open the steel case that contained a hundred connectors. At a time like this he needed a specialist who would have known exactly what each connector and wire was for. All he could do was try to foul up the system.

He was fouling up four houses at least, but in the middle of the night none of the sleeping families in the neighborhood was likely to discover the problem. In the morning the phone company would have its problem. He cut no wires, just moved them around from connector to connector, until—as he judged—he had totally screwed up the telephone system for the Frenchi house and every house around it.

Then Bolan identified—easily enough—the wires that supplied electrical power to the Frenchi house. From a pouch on his belt he took a paper-wrapped package of thermal plastique. He unwrapped it and pressed the doughy substance onto the wire, making a ball. Then from another pouch he removed a small electronic device—a radio-controlled detonator. When the signal was received, it would ignite the thermal plastique, and a few seconds later the intense heat of the plastique would burn through the wire and cut off electricity to the Frenchi house.

Back on the ground he handed Bonnie the transmitter.

"Not until I tell you," he warned. "The lights will go out only when it's to our best advantage."

"Okay. Now we go in? How?"

Bolan shook his head. "No, not now. Now we make ourselves scarce for half an hour. If the work I just did has alerted somebody, we don't want to be making our entry just when help arrives. We wait."

WAITING WAS the hardest part. They stationed themselves at one end of the block—Bolan in the alley, the other two on the street—and watched for police or private security men to arrive.

From time to time, Bonnie ran to Bolan, saying that she and Lug had seen nothing, so when could they move? Bolan kept shaking his head. When he judged enough time had passed, Bolan slipped out of the alley and signaled for Bonnie and Lug to join him.

"The only way to go, as far as I can see, is up on the roof."

Lug peered up at the steep-slanted slate roof of the nineteenth-century house. It was a dull gray color in the light of a moon that only half shone through the thin cover of drifting low cloud. Bonnie stared, too. Both of them were obviously skeptical of their ability to climb.

Bolan led them into the alley. The wall behind the Frenchi house was made of red brick, and was eight feet high. It was, though, the same kind of wall that surrounded all the other tiny backyards in the neighborhood—it wasn't topped with wire or broken glass. That would have been conspicuous. On the other hand, it might have been topped with fine trip wires or other sensors, and Bolan was reluctant to touch it.

For a like reason he wouldn't touch the green board gate in the single opening in the wall, where the household put trash cans out in the alley.

He glanced up. His glob of thermal plastique was as visible as if a fist were clenched around the wire. But a person had to know where it was and what it was in order to see it.

"All right," he said quietly. "Where we're going is up on the neighbor's wall. If that's booby-trapped, we're in trouble. If it isn't, it'll give us access to that old oak in the neighbor's yard, and from there we can make it the rest of the way. Lug, give me a boost."

Lug clasped his hands, and when he had Bolan's foot in his cupped palms he hoisted the warrior into the air. Bolan snatched at the top of the neighbor's wall, found a handhold and dragged himself up.

No response. No alarm.

The top of the brick wall was about eight inches wide, which was too narrow to crawl on. Bolan stood. Balancing himself carefully, he prowled in a crouch along the top of the wall until he was at the big old oak. He tossed a weighted length of line over a limb, watched the weight loop around the branch, then tugged and tightened the line. In one fluid movement, he swung into the lower limbs of the tree and became nearly invisible, concealed by the leaves.

He untangled his rope. Climbing a little higher, he secured one end of the rope to a branch and tossed the weighted end over the wall.

In a moment Lug was on top of the wall. Then he threw himself off the wall and swung hard against the tree trunk, just below the lowest limb. He grunted as he hit the tree, then recovered and scrambled up, scuffing the trunk with his shoes and hauling himself up the rope.

Bonnie tried the maneuver. She didn't know enough to hold her feet thrust forward and hit the trunk squarely, falling to the ground.

Bolan was beside her in an instant. He snatched her up, and with Lug tugging on the line, carried her up into the cover of the leaves.

The woman was weak from the impact; the wind had been knocked out of her.

"Transmitter . . . ?" Bolan whispered in her ear.

"I have it," she replied.

He nodded. Leaving her behind with Lug, who would hold her until she recovered her breath and strength, Bolan climbed higher in the tree.

From the sturdy limbs of the tall oak it wasn't difficult to reach the roof of the neighbor's house. The roof was steep, and the slates were slippery. He sat astride a dormer and attached a rope to a vent pipe. When his two team members climbed over, he didn't want them to fall.

Bonnie came over first, grabbing the rope and making her way confidently to the peak of the roof. Then came Lug. In two minutes the three of them clung to the top ridge, looking down on the roof of the Frenchi house.

The windows were dark in the dormers on the steep roof, but lights shone dimly from lower windows.

The two houses were separated by no more than ten feet. The brick wall surrounded both, but their backyards were separated only by a wrought-iron fence. Other houses up and down the street had their own walls, but these two were within the one brick wall, as if they had once been joint property. Bonnie said Frenchi had no contact with the doctor who lived in this house.

"All we have to do is go across," Bolan whispered. "Equipment check."

He checked his own as his two soldiers checked theirs. Until now they had eyeballed the night—except when he had used his night goggles while he was on the utility pole—but now he lowered the Gundersons over his eyes and adjusted them. The dimly lighted night scene turned abruptly bright, illuminated in greenish but radiant light.

"Okay, troops. Time to move on to enemy territory."

Bolan looped the nylon rope over the vent pipe and lowered himself down the steep slope until he could fix his feet in the old copper gutter along the lower edge of the roof. Then he pulled the rope down and tossed it across the gap between the two houses. On the fifth try, he managed to get a loop over the vent pipe that rose above the master bathroom.

He looked down. The ten-foot space between the two houses was filled with shrubs that were stunted from lack of light. The muddy ground around them would be a hard landing for someone falling twenty feet. He had no doubt of his own ability, but had to think about how Lug and Bonnie would cross.

Clutching the rope, the warrior swung across. His extended feet thumped hard against the brick wall of the Frenchi house. He hauled himself up and scrambled onto the roof.

No alarms. Whatever electronics were used, no one had installed alarm sensors on the roof.

Bolan sat down, his feet pressed against the eaves, and went over his weapons once more. The Heckler & Koch would be his main weapon inside, and he ran the final check carefully.

The problem now was to get Bonnie across. Bolan planted his feet and tossed the rope back. He indicated with gestures that she should tie the rope around her waist. He wasn't sure why she was so intent on being a part of this. The money she had taken off Al Felucci's body would take care of her for a long time. She was free of Frenchi, and she had no habit. She was still young, still good-looking. He could only believe something burned in her gut the way it did in his.

He ended his pointless musing and wrapped the end of the rope around his left arm. Responding to his gestures, Bonnie slid down the roof next door. When he pulled the rope tight, she let herself fall.

The woman swung across and hit the wall. She was learning—this time she hit with the soles of her shoes. In a moment Bonnie was beside him on the roof of the Frenchi house, helping him loosen the rope.

"IF THE ALARM SYSTEM works on the attic windows, we're in trouble," Bonnie whispered as Bolan ran a glass cutter across a pane on a dormer window.

"Just be sure your damned gun's ready," Lug muttered.

Bolan had already pressed his face to the glass and scanned the attic through his Gundersons. He had seen nothing. The attic was empty, except for some wooden crates that looked as though they'd stood there for years.

The glass snapped, and he pressed it in. It fell inside and landed on a floor covered with a quarter-inch-thick layer of dust, which muffled its impact. Bolan reached inside and found a latch, which he turned, then pushed hard. The dormer window swung open.

Bolan crawled through first. Again, nothing. Whatever sensors were present in this house had been installed by someone who hadn't anticipated entry from the attic.

"Bonnie," Bolan whispered, "there's the fold-up stairs. Where does that come down?"

"In the hall," she said. "In the hall with the main staircase. Right above the door to the bathroom."

"Which means to get to Frenchi, you have to charge down that hall and—"

"The first left," she said.

"The master bedroom."

"Right."

Bolan surveyed the attic. In a house this old, the attic had a firm floor. You couldn't just jump off a beam and drop into a room, breaking through the drywall. The dusty floor beneath his feet was strong wood.

He crept across the floor to the drop-down steps. They were meant to be pulled down from below. He pushed, and they swung down.

The hall below was brightly lighted. He could see the stairs coming up from the first floor. To his right, facing the front of the house, was a door. Bonnie's sketch, which he had memorized, said that was a bedroom. The door to his left opened into a bathroom. Ahead was a lateral hallway.

The house was quiet.

Bolan gestured, checked his H&K once more, then dropped down, followed by Bonnie and Lug.

They stood in the upper hall, at the intersection of a lopsided T.

Bolan looked at Bonnie and pointed at a door.

"Frenchi?" he whispered.

She nodded.

Lug slipped up alongside Bolan. "Something's wrong with this," he muttered. "How the hell did we get in the middle of the fort and see no soldiers?"

Bolan shook his head.

Lug persisted. "That Frenchi's bedroom?" he asked, nodding toward the door to their left. "Uh-uh. Somethin' screwy. Too goddamned easy."

Bolan turned to Bonnie. He thought for a moment, then said, "Turn out their lights."

She pressed the button on the transmitter, igniting the thermal plastique on the 220-volt line leading into the house. After half a minute the house went dark. For a second. The emergency lights, battery powered, came on immediately. What was worse, the failure of electric power in the house set off the alarm system.

Hardmen charged out of the bedroom that was their dormitory. Presuming the threat came from the first floor, they ran for the stairs, carrying heavy weapons. Lug Lugano had no hesitancy about firing on them, and his H&K chopped them down as they burst through the door.

Bonnie had set her Beretta to fire 3-round bursts—she had learned the nuances of the weapon during the afternoon and was much better equipped, mentally, to use it than she had been when she used the Walther to kill Felucci. She held her fire. Lugano had cut down the first few men out of the bedroom.

The woman had underestimated the number of wise guys Frenchi had summoned to protect him. Three men lay dead, and others, seeing how their friends had fallen in the doorway, backed into the dormitory, demolishing the walls with sprays of 9 mm slugs.

Bolan searched for the emergency light and took the unit out with one quick, short burst of his H&K.

There were many emergency-light units in the house, though, and knocking out one only darkened the upper hall. Another shone in the hardmen's bedroom, and still others lighted the house downstairs.

The hardmen in the bedroom didn't have to risk stepping into the door to fire. Streams of slugs chopped through the old plaster wall. Bolan's team retreated out of the line of fire, backing along the hall and through the open door to the bathroom. The corridor filled with the dust of the shattered plaster.

A girl screamed.

"Clara..." Bonnie muttered.

"Tell her to say where she is," Bolan said.

"She doesn't speak English."

"Clara!" Bolan shouted. *"Mi ascolti! Si metta a pavimento. Presto! Pericolo!"*

Another burst of 9 mm slugs ripped through the walls.

Bolan knelt in the bathroom door and fired a stream of parabellums into the already shattered wall of the hardmen's bedroom. Someone in the room shrieked—hit in the legs, likely, since Bolan had fired low.

A couple of slugs punched through the plaster of the wall between the hall and the master bedroom, pistol shots. They had been aimed blindly, but one slug zipped between Bolan and Bonnie, and hit the toilet, blowing water all over the bathroom. Lug loosed a burst toward the fist-sized holes made by the pistol slugs.

"Careful," Bolan cautioned. "I want Frenchi alive."

Bonnie, flat on the bathroom floor, inched forward into the door and fired her Beretta toward the sagging wall of the hardmen's bedroom.

Suddenly, the bathroom wall behind them shattered. It had been blasted by a charge of heavy pellets from a big shotgun, a *lupara*. The first blast was followed immediately by a second one. The wall collapsed, leaving a ragged man-sized hole. A hardman shoved the muzzle of an Uzi through the opening. Both Bolan and Lug fired on him, and before he could pull his trigger, the guy was hit head and chest with two deadly torrents of parabellums. Thrown backward by the shock of so much metal, the shredded corpse hung for a moment on the windowsill at the head of the stairs before it slipped down, leaving a bloody smear on window and wall.

As Bolan jammed another magazine into his H&K, another shotgun blast blew away more of the bathroom wall, the pellets spraying the room. Bonnie shrieked. Two or three pellets had punched through the skin of her left shoulder, leaving small, bloody wounds.

The shotgun roared again, and Bolan felt the agonizing sting of pellets striking his back. He jerked a grenade off his webbing, pulled the pin and tossed the metal orb underhand through the hole in the wall. He threw himself over Bonnie to push her to the floor. Lug dropped flat.

Men screamed and threw themselves down the stairs, but they didn't escape the agonizing death Bolan had thrown to them. The MU-50 went off with a muffled roar, blasting a deadly storm of razor-sharp needles through the hall and stairwell.

Bolan scrambled to his feet and jumped through the hole. He held the H&K ready to take on all comers, but the four hardmen on the stairs weren't moving. Their clothes and bodies were bloody shreds. The big sawed-off shotgun lay beside one of the corpses.

An Uzi slid across the floor of the hall, tossed from the bedroom from which the first gunfire had come. The wise guy inside was surrendering.

"Okay," Bolan ordered, "crawl out."

Lug stood in the bathroom door, his H&K leveled on the door to the bedroom. The hardman crawled out, dragging his wounded legs.

"Anybody else?" Bolan asked.

The man shook his head, glancing back into the room.

"All right. Frenchi?"

The hardman shook his head again. "Frenchi ain't here," he muttered.

Bolan nodded toward the master bedroom. "Who's in there?" he asked.

"Sal," the man replied.

Bolan stepped to the hole in the bathroom wall. "Stay in there and out of sight," he said in a low tone to Bonnie. "Salvatore Balestrino is here, and we don't want him to see you."

He stepped past the wounded man, then moved along the main hall to the door of the master bedroom.

"You want to come out, Sally? Or do we come and get you?"

"I'm openin' the door."

He opened it and stood, facing Bolan. Salvatore Balestrino was a senior citizen of the Mob. Gray, wrinkled, he thought of himself as a man who could no longer be surprised.

"Hello, Sally," Bolan said. "Where's your boss?"

Balestrino shook his head. "I don't know."

"If I believed that, I'd believe in the tooth fairy."

"I can't help what you believe or don't believe," the mobster replied. "And you can do whatever you want to do about it. I don't know where the son of a bitch is. He left me here to take the heat. And went . . . I don't know where."

"Where are Janice and Brenda Elliott?"

"If I knew, he wouldn't have left me here so I could tell you."

Bolan stepped past the aging mobster and entered the master bedroom. As he had guessed, a frightened young woman lay in the bed, covered by the sheet and quietly weeping. The wall behind and just above the bed was shattered by Lug's short burst of slugs, his reply to Sally's pistol shots.

"How you going to explain all this, Sally?" Bolan asked when he returned to the doorway.

Balestrino favored him with a sarcastic grin. "Somebody doesn't like us."

"Your boss shot a finger at the Commission," Bolan said.

"Glad you told me. Thanks. That's what I'll tell the cops."

Lug appeared in the bedroom door.

"Figure we oughta move on, Mack. This job hasn't been what you'd call quiet."

"Check downstairs," Bolan replied. "Check the cellar."

10

Janice Elliott groaned and struggled to sit up on her mattress. She was in pain and so was Brenda. They had lain all night with their hands cuffed behind their backs. Their shoulders ached, and their wrists stung where the tight steel had rubbed the skin off.

"You've gotta do it, Mom," Brenda whispered. "It's not going to make any difference."

"I though they'd come back in an hour or so. I didn't imagine they'd leave us all night."

Brenda rolled over, jerking her mother's ankle—they were still chained together. "Gotta do it..." she breathed.

"If they ever come back and ask," Janice added.

"SPEND AN UNCOMFORTABLE night, ladies?" Cesare Frenchi taunted.

Janice looked up at the man she guessed had ordered the death of her husband. He was half a man, she told herself scornfully, no more than half the man Ron had been. This mobster, whose name she hadn't been told, was short, a rather flabby little man with a sadistic leer on his ugly face.

"Ready to do your job?" he asked.

Janice nodded.

Frenchi shook his head. "You spent a miserable night for nothing," he jeered.

It was best to say nothing. She blinked and sighed.

"Okay," he said brusquely to the two hardmen who were with him. "Get the ladies cleaned up. Let them clean their pigpen here first, then put them in a shower. I'll see them when they don't stink."

"LOOK AT THIS," Terranova yelled. He was sitting in the kitchen, watching television.

The pictures on the screen showed the Frenchi house in Boston. The street was crowded with emergency vehicles, and the camera focused on the front door as police carried out body bags, one after another. A television reporter gave all the details.

"Left alive in the house of carnage were just four people—Salvatore Balestrino, who police say is a lifelong mafioso, two women, Clara Albanesi and Laura Dickerson, and a wounded man, Antonio Venosa, who police say has a criminal record for theft and extortion. Balestrino, who has been on parole from a life sentence for murder, was jailed for parole violations, including possession of a handgun. The Albanesi woman, who does not speak English, was held as an illegal immigrant. Venosa is listed in fair condition this morning, suffering from bullet wounds to the legs. The Dickerson woman was questioned and released.

"The explanation for the deadly battle in which hundreds of rounds of ammunition were fired inside the Frenchi house, is unclear. It seems to involve an attack by a rival gang.

"Police say they have long suspected that the owner of the house, Cesare Frenchi, is a Mafia capo. The presence in the house last night of a dozen heavily armed bodyguards, nearly all of whom died in the attack, would seem to prove at least that the house is not an ordinary family home.

"Their assailants escaped. Neighbors, who sneaked occasional peeks from their windows at intervals during the firefight, say that no more than three attackers, carrying heavy weapons, dashed from the house after the attack and made their getaway in a dark sedan. Of course, some of the dead might be attackers, not defenders.

"State and federal officers this morning joined the investigation into this spectacular gang battle."

Frenchi stared at the television set, clenching and unclenching his fists as the camera moved inside and showed the wreckage of his home.

"We shouldn't have left Clara there," he muttered to Terranova. "The Albanesi family will be nosed off if the Feds send her back to Sicily. I got enough troubles without that."

"Bolan..." Terranova began.

"Yeah, Bolan," Frenchi snapped.

"All those guys! I mean, how could he...? What kind of guy is this Bolan that he can take out that many made men? And how'd he get in? How'd he—"

"Shut up," Frenchi growled.

"We gotta get Sally out," Terranova said. "Who we got on the pad?"

Frenchi tossed back his head. "Hah! Sally's the guy who *knows* who we got on the pad. He'll take care of himself. He has to sit tight for a while. If he gets himself out too soon—"

"Okay. But who's *consigliere* until he comes back?"

"What? *You* want to be?"

"Well—"

"Okay, Guido. You're *consigliere*. So what's your advice?"

The dark, brutal-looking Terranova was genuinely affected by his appointment, offhand and temporary though it was. He frowned and pondered. "Bolan..." he began hesitantly. "We gotta stop Bolan. And, well, I think we've gotta make peace with the Commission."

"Peace with the Commission, huh? Well, to make peace with Clean Joe Rossi we've got to give up the two women. Then what do we have to use against Bolan?"

"He isn't falling for it," Terranova murmured.

"So far," Frenchi said. "Maybe if I send him a *real* finger, say from the daughter. Yeah, I'll send him the daughter's finger—in ice. Hmm? What then?"

"Then you got one hostage instead of two and still no Bolan."

Cesare Frenchi scowled. "Remember this, Guido," he said. "Nobody—and I mean *nobody*—gets away with what Bolan's so far got away with. The Sugar was his friend. The wife is his friend. If I get nothing else out of this, I'll have the satisfaction of sending Bolan two corpses. I get Bolan, or Bolan gets two bodies. Remember that."

THE MOBSTER HAD HAD to unlock the chain that linked Janice's ankle to Brenda's. Otherwise they couldn't have taken off their urine-soaked clothes. He wouldn't let them close the shower curtain, and he'd sat and smirked as they showered. When the women were clean and dry, he handed them two big blue chambray shirts and chained them together again. The shirt just covered Janice's hips, though Brenda's covered her a little better.

Being taken out of the basement had afforded them a brief view out the windows of the house. They could see the ocean. The house was somewhere on the coast, on high ground above the sea, but it was impossible to say where. They had traveled by air, so it wasn't anywhere near Baltimore or Washington. Maine, perhaps. Or even somewhere on Long Island.

During their night of misery they had fouled the floor, not their mattresses, so all they'd had to do to clean up was to wipe the floor with wet paper towels. The hardman returned them to their room, where they sat despondently in the vinyl-covered armchairs. Brenda wept softly.

"All right," Frenchi barked when he returned. "What I want is a letter to Mack Bolan. He's the one giving me all this grief."

Janice nodded, feeling, for the first time, a glimmer of hope. She remembered Bolan as a man of integrity and compassion, a man with a deep sense of justice. She and Brenda just might survive after all.

"You write your own words. Whatever you want to say. Then I'll read it."

She wrote:

Dear Mack,

It's me, no question. You remember the night we had lobster at King's Court? That was the last time you, Ron and I were together. Happier times for all of us. Right now I'm held prisoner by a man whose name I don't know, at a place I don't know. I don't know why, but I imagine you do. What he wants me to tell you is that he has me and Brenda and that he will kill us if you don't do what he wants. My judgment is that he means it. So I don't know what to say to you. If it were just me, I'd say one thing, and I guess you know what that is. But it's not just me. He has Brenda here, too. He's handing me a newspaper. I guess that's so he can take another Polaroid of us, the way he did before, and you will know we were alive after the day that paper came out. So that's it. You'll have to use your own judgment, Mack. We'll accept that, no matter what it is.

Janice

"THERE'S AN IMPORTANT CLUE here," Hal Brognola said.

The big Fed had flown to Boston and sat with Bolan in a motel room in Watertown. Bolan believed in moving his headquarters often, and he had moved into this modest little place and put Bonnie and Lug in another motel a mile away. Bolan and Bonnie had had shotgun pellets dug out of their backs by a doctor sent by DiRosario, and the warrior wore no shirt over the wide bandage taped to his upper back and shoulders.

"I see the clue," Bolan concurred. "The newspaper before was the *Boston Globe*. This one's the *Boston Globe*. Unless Brother Frenchi is smart enough to buy an out-of-town paper to fool us, he's holding Janice and Brenda somewhere not too far from here."

"The *Globe* has wide circulation," Brognola reminded. "On the other hand, it is carrier delivered only in a reasonably restricted area. And this is carrier delivered, I'd judge."

"Because it's yesterday's paper and these pictures were delivered today."

"Well, there's no mailing label on that paper," Brognola said. "Of course it could have been bought in a newsstand that sells out-of-town papers. It seems likely, though, that Frenchi has our two women somewhere in the area where the *Globe* is tossed in the driveway."

"In Boston, you think?" Bolan asked. He squinted over the two Polaroid pictures showing Janice and Brenda holding up the front page of the newspaper.

"No. It's possible, but I don't think so. We put these pictures under a microscope. Fortunately Polaroid film has very fine grain, and these pictures are well focused. Under high magnification it's possible to make out the stories, at least the headlines on the upper half of the paper. We compared the *Globe* in the pictures with samples we got from the newspaper office. This newspaper is an early press run. They pulled the third-column story and substituted a breaking story during the night, after the first press run."

"And most of the early run goes on trucks to out-of-town subscribers," Bolan concluded.

Brognola nodded. "The first run goes on the street in Boston, and a few papers are sold by street vendors. Most of the run goes on trucks like you say. Not just out to the suburbs. To the far reaches of the paper's carrier-delivery area."

"Meaning?"

"Meaning this paper was probably delivered twenty-five miles, minimum, outside Boston."

"A big territory," Bolan conceded.

"Not as big as it was before they gave us this clue. The clue doesn't absolutely eliminate Boston itself, but it probably does. I'd say the two women are in New England, somewhere outside Boston."

"Unless Frenchi was clever enough to fly Boston papers down to Maryland, to throw us off."

Brognola stepped to the window of the motel room and looked out at the shimmering heat rising off the asphalt of the parking lot. Sunlight flashing off automobile windshields struck his eyes. It was uncomfortable, so he returned to his chair.

"I want to divide the work this way," he said to Bolan. "Let me handle the search for Ron's wife and daughter. I can work within all the rules on that. I'll let the FBI handle most of it. They'll recruit help from all the state and local police forces."

"And I'll keep the heat on Frenchi."

Brognola sighed. "Yeah. We can't forget there's a terrible risk in that."

"There's no alternative," Bolan said grimly. "I learned a long time ago that you can't surrender to hostage takers. The only way to handle them is tighten the screws. They have to be made to understand that harming the hostages will hurt them more than anything else they can do. Frenchi has a cause, and it's just as good a cause as any claimed by PLO or IRA terrorists. He wants to save the little empire he's building. Well, every day he holds those two women, he's going to lose just that much more."

"I wish we could handle terrorist hostage-taking that way," Brognola growled.

"You could," Bolan stated coldly, "if anyone in a high enough place had the guts."

As THE SUN SANK toward the horizon, Bolan waited on the ramp outside the Dundee Aviation hangar at Boston Logan International. A constant stream of aircraft sank out of the darker sky to the east, lights flashing, and settled onto the active runway. Evening was one of the busy times for an airport as big as this. The birds were coming home, filled with East Coast businessmen who left on flights that carried them away early in the morning and brought them back late in the evening.

Most of the old prop-driven freight planes would come in later. But Bolan—in the guise of Major Morrison and still taken for an FAA inspector—had checked the board in the Dundee office and knew Russ Caldwell would be bringing the DC-6 in during the rush hour.

Bolan had a little hand-held radio tuned to the tower frequency, and he listened to the chatter as the controllers called aircraft into the pattern and cleared them to the runway.

"Uh, DC-6 Four-five Delta, turn final now. Cleared to land. Expedite as much as you can, sir. I have turbine traffic behind you."

"Four-five Delta, Roger. Will expedite. Will slow up on short final, for the quick turn off your runway."

"Thank you, Four-five. Appreciate that."

Bolan watched the DC-6 touch down and swing off the runway. It taxied a long way, then turned onto the ramp. Ground men rushed around with light-sticks, guiding the big aircraft into place, and finally Caldwell shut down the engines and switched off the marker lights.

Bolan extended his hand to Caldwell as he came down the steps.

Caldwell brushed past. "Don't need to talk to you."

Bolan grabbed him by the arm. "What's going on?" he demanded.

"Check the boss," Caldwell snapped angrily. "You know what happened to Tom?"

"No, I don't. I guess we can't talk here. Let's go."

"IT DOESN'T MAKE any difference whether he had anything to do with it or not," Caldwell said an hour later in a bar in Southie. "They sent a leg breaker. Just because it happened in our hangar. You busted up their tomato-coke shipment, spoiled their stuff and they worked over Tom Dundee. He'll be okay, sort of. Broken arm, broken leg. He's lucky to be alive."

"What about you?"

Caldwell shook his head. "We check the DC-6 from end to end, top to bottom, every time we take off. They could do it, you know—I mean sabotage the airplane. If you read in the papers that I went down with a DC-6 in the mountains somewhere, it won't be an accident."

"All it needed was—"

"All it needed was that it happened in our hangar," Caldwell interrupted. "That's all it needed. Every operator on the airport knows it. That's how they work—by keeping people scared to death."

"That's why it's so perfectly obvious how things happen, yet nobody stops it," Bolan said. "The tomatoes . . . You knew the coke was in them—or you guessed. Tom Dundee knew—or guessed."

"So do the airport cops. Some are on the pad. Most of them are scared of what will happen to their families if they make a bust. Me? If anybody guesses who you are and knows I'm talking to you—"

"There's only one way to be safe, Russ."

Caldwell nodded. "Put more muscle to them than they put to you. Only before *you* came, nobody could."

"I know a place in Virginia, Russ. If you've got a family, why don't you fly them down there for a week or so? There's a landing strip near the Farm. Nobody's going to touch them there. I promise you that. I'll show you the place on the chart, and you can fly them there tonight. Some friends of mine will meet you."

"A week or so?"

Bolan nodded. "For sure."

Caldwell frowned. "You're damn serious, aren't you?"

"I want the name of the guy who broke Dundee's leg. You tell me, and I'll go home with you and help you get your family safely to the plane you'll fly to Virginia. Then I'm going after the leg-breaker."

"HEAT!" Antonin Cipirello yelled. He tossed the newspaper across the room, then threw a glass of wine at the television set. "Dummy! Cesare's an idiot! *Idiot!*"

Two hardmen were sitting in the booth with him. This kind of talk made them nervous. Cesare Frenchi wasn't a don—he wasn't old enough to be called that, and he was a generation removed from Sicily—but he was the head of the Family. He was the man who had made Cipirello, and they knew Tony wouldn't talk that way if Cesare had been sitting there.

"Yeah, you guys," Cipirello said. "I know what you're thinkin'. Well, Cesare's not so tough. He's not so smart, either. He fingered a Sugar. Dumb! Now he's snatched the Sugar's wife and daughter, which has brought the Commission down on our heads, plus it's brought down this Bolan. Cesare's..." He paused. "Cesare's off his rocker."

His two wise guys looked down into their glasses of beer. They didn't like this talk, but neither would contradict Cipirello. Guys got hurt that way.

By anybody's standards, Antonin Cipirello was a big man, six foot four or five, broad shouldered, muscular. There was something threatening in the way he carried himself—shoulders back, his head switching constantly from side to side, his glance switching, too, as if he were nervously alert for something that might come at him from either side. He wasn't Sicilian, from the look of him, his men judged. More likely a Tuscan or Venetian. His light brown hair was curly, and his eyes were pale blue. He was also handsome. Girls hung around him as if he was a rock star.

Cipirello had a short fuse. When he hurt people, he hurt them bad, which was why he was a valued member of Frenchi's Family. The capo always had to talk to him, like an uncle, before he went out on a job. "Hold your temper, Tony. Break enough bones to make the guy remember, but don't kill him. If I want a hit, I'll say hit. If I want legs broken, I'll say that."

One of the wise guys—his name was Carlo—had a mouse under his eye right now. He'd tapped Cipirello on the shoulder while he'd been working over Dundee to remind him of what Frenchi had said, and Cipirello had turned and swung on *him*.

Carlo resented that. He stared glumly into his beer, but he had resolved to report to his capo every word Cipirello had uttered.

As far as Carlo was concerned, Tony's criticism of Cesare rang false. They had more in common than any other two men he knew—uncontrollable temper, ambition that knew no limits, complete indifference to anyone else's feelings and an elemental brutality that even Family men found hard to understand.

Carlo had thought of killing Tony. Maybe he would someday if he ever saw the opportunity.

CALDWELL HAD SAID the leg breaker hung out in a bar in Southie, among the Irish. It didn't fit, but that was what the flyer had said, based on what he knew. Bolan had to accept it. He had no other idea where to find Tony Cipirello.

He had sent Russ Caldwell and his family to Stony Man Farm. They'd accept him and help him, as they had accepted and helped Dick and Lynn Greenberg, without asking where they had met the one-time head of the Phoenix Project. The connection was severed, but the kinship couldn't be. Officially, the Farm knew nothing of Mack Bolan. Unofficially its occupants offered to help and succor whenever it was needed, no questions asked.

The warrior had picked up a Red Sox cap and a Red Sox satin jacket—the latter at a thrift shop, so it was a little frayed and stained. The jacket concealed his Beretta 93-R.

The bar was dark and the air stank of beer and cigarette smoke. Like a lot of Southie bars, it was a place a stranger wasn't welcome. Everyone knew someone else. No one was drinking alone.

Bolan stepped to the bar. "Beer," he growled to the bartender. "Miller."

The bartender popped the cap off a bottle and shoved it across the bar, as well as a glass still wet from a quick dunk in detergent and a swished rinse. Bolan picked up the bottle and took a long drink.

"Suppose to be meeting someone here," Bolan said. "Laura Dickerson. You know her?"

The bartender shook his head and moved down the bar.

Two young men stood beside Bolan at the bar—two beefy, redheaded Irish lads dressed in dirty blue jeans and dirty white T-shirts, with plastic caps on their heads. They talked and gradually they muscled Bolan, moving slowly toward him until one of them pressed hard against Bolan's hip. Neither man looked up. They just kept edging more and more against Bolan, seeing whether they could force him to move. It was a game, obviously. Someone probably played it with every stranger.

Okay, so Bolan would play.

The man closest to the warrior bumped him, then again. Bolan didn't move, didn't turn to look at his antagonist. He moved his foot, placing his heel squarely on the man's instep. Then he shifted from his other foot, letting all his weight down, heel to instep.

"Hey! What the hell do you think you're doing, fella?"

"Sorry," Bolan said quietly, and reached for the man's hand as though to shake it. He closed his hand in a viselike grip.

The redhead flushed with pain as Bolan's steely muscles crushed his fingers.

The Executioner let go. "Nice to have met you," he said with a wry smile.

The two bullies backed away.

The bartender had been watching, and now Bolan turned to him. "I asked you if you knew Laura Dickerson."

"No, I don't. Don't think I ever heard the name."

Bolan raised his beer and drank deeply. "A friend of Tony's," he continued. "Tony Cipirello."

The bartender shrugged, as if the name meant nothing to him, but Bolan saw his eye shift toward a booth opposite the bar. Bolan could see the booth in the mirror behind the bartender, and he could see three men. One of them looked like the leg breaker Caldwell had described—a big, square-jawed, curly haired fellow. The other two men were smaller, darker, weaselly.

The bartender wasn't sly nor smart. Within a minute he had gone to the booth to tell the big man that the stranger at the bar had mentioned his name. Bolan kept his back to the booth, but he stood where he could see it reflected in the mirror. The three men stared at him.

Bolan shoved money across the bar to pay for the beer, then turned and walked to the booth.

"Cipirello," he said coldly to the big man.

Antonin Cipirello took his measure for a moment, then said, "Who the hell are you?"

"It doesn't make any difference who I am," Bolan replied. "You leaned on a friend of mine, and I don't like it."

"Who gives a damn what you like?" Cipirello sneered. He reached inside his jacket and began to draw a revolver.

Bolan waited until he was sure what was coming out of Cipirello's jacket, then he drew the Beretta, put the muzzle close to the bridge of Cipirello's nose and pulled the trigger.

The Beretta coughed quietly. People near the booth didn't notice the sound, but Cipirello's brains splattered against the wall behind him.

Bolan's eyes bored through the remaining mobsters. "Tell Frenchi to score one more for the Feds."

He walked out of the bar and was on the street before anyone but the two terrified men in the booth realized that Tony Cipirello had been hit.

11

Midnight. The van marked with the name and logo of the airport police pulled away from the hangar belonging to Shamrock Air Cargo. Bolan, wearing his Gundersons, had watched the fake cops load eighteen cases into the van—cocaine hidden inside something. He had watched and listened. How much coke? Who could tell? Maybe a million dollars' worth, judging from the cases he had watched being loaded into the van.

The warrior had stepped outside and made a signal as the van swung around the corner of the hangar. And there it shrieked to a stop.

A young woman—a good-looking young woman, stark naked—stood in the glow of the headlights. The two mobsters jumped out of the van, grinning. One man trotted toward her, while the other walked after him, laughing.

Bonnie had concealed the Beretta behind her back. She shot the closer man first, then the other—two muffled pops. As she walked to the corner of the hangar and picked up her clothes from the top of a trash bin, Bolan tossed a phosphorous grenade into the back of the van.

THE SHARK HAD LEANED hard on the citizen, and chuckled to himself as he walked along the Cambridge street. He'd collected a thousand in principal and a thousand in vig, and the citizen still owed four thousand and would owe another thousand in vig by the end of the week. It was a damned good business.

The way it worked, he'd provided the capital originally—ten thousand to put out in loans—and for the right to work the territory, plus help in enforcing, he handed Frenchi's collector half the vig. My God! Half the vig! The vigorish he took on loans was ten times what a loan company would take, and after paying Frenchi, he had five times left. Besides which, Frenchi gave him protection. The guy who'd tried to muscle in on his territory had had an accident. The citizen who'd gone to the cops had had an accident—because the cops he'd gone to were on Frenchi's pad.

What a business! The shark, whose name was Briggs, had parlayed his original ten thousand dollars into more than a million and a quarter—*after* taking care of Frenchi.

If he had a problem—and any business had its problems—it was that Cesare Frenchi was . . . How to put it? Unstable. The heat from the newspapers had to be followed by heat from the cops. He couldn't understand what the capo had in mind. The word was, he'd wasted a Sugar.

Well, if Frenchi had thought it was necessary, then it was necessary. Nobody had ever had it so good as they'd had it under Cesare Frenchi.

He reached his white Cadillac, got in and sat down. Frenchi's man was late. So, okay, he'd wait.

There he was. Gutsy. That laundry bag he carried—looking like a Harvardian carrying dirty clothes to the Laundromat—was full of money. The loan shark had never caught the young fellow's name, had never asked. It was really none of his business. He was a collector, the young fellow. A tall boy, blond, with conspicuous acne scars on his colorless, long-jawed face. It was a sober face. The collector never smiled; his eyes rarely moved; he could somehow speak and hardly move his mouth. He was a brutal-looking boy, menacing.

The shark had never had any trouble with him. He wondered what would happen if he ever did. No hassle, probably. The hassle would come from the bone crusher, later.

What was odd was how accurately the collector guessed how much the take had been. It was as if he spent a lot of time in the neighborhood, asking questions, checking up on things. The truth was, the guy was what he looked like, a Harvard student. He had some kind of . . . Well, what would you call it? He *knew* how much a shark in this neighborhood should collect. He wasn't unreasonable, but he was uncannily right—and demanding.

The collector walked up to the Cadillac. ''I figure I've got an envelope of about fifteen coming, right?'' he said.

That was how it always was—never a word of greeting, never a word about how's your health or how do you like the weather—just business, quick and straight.

''Eighteen.''

He did this sometimes. It never hurt to hand over a little more than necessary. Three thousand extra. What the hell? He wouldn't be surprised if the collector ripped off the extra. Which was okay, too. A little investment in goodwill wasn't a bad idea.

He handed over his envelope, a big yellow one stuffed with bills. The collector dropped it into his laundry bag, where it fell among two dozen other envelopes, the take from a lot of other businesses. Briggs saw the other envelopes, and his wasn't the fattest. He'd never dare ask, but he guessed the Family had had a good night.

The collector pulled tight the string that closed the laundry bag. He nodded. That was it. That was as much acknowledgement of their long business relationship as he ever extended. He would now turn away and walk down a dark street, where a score of people knew what was in that bag, and no one would touch him. No one would dare. Briggs had heard grisly stories of what happened to the last guy who did dare.

"Gentlemen."

Neither of them had noticed the big man who had stepped up behind the collector as he stood, bent over the Cadillac, receiving the envelope and speaking his few words to Briggs. Briggs could see him—a tough-looking man with scars on his face, dressed in a blue suit with a white shirt and tie. He could also see the automatic in his right hand.

The collector glanced at the man and the pistol. His expression didn't change. "You're making a mistake," he said.

"No," Lug Lugano contradicted. "No mistake. Just put the bag down on the sidewalk."

"That's the property of Cesare Frenchi," the collector warned.

"That's right," Lugano said agreeably.

"You touch what's his—"

The collector stopped, and at last his expression changed. His mouth dropped open. The big man with the scarred face was pouring a big can of lighter fluid into the laundry bag, onto the envelopes stuffed with money. As the collector and the shark gaped, Lugano snapped a cigarette lighter and tossed it, flaming, into the bag.

The bag whooshed and began to burn fiercely, generating thick black smoke.

The collector shook his head. "You're a dead man."

"Frenchi's a dead man," Lugano replied. "You remember my name, and when you tell him what happened, tell him it was Umberto Lugano who burned his envelopes. Umberto Lugano. You got that? A man of respect. Not some two-bit punk like Cesare Frenchi."

"You're in serious trouble," the collector mumbled.

"No, you're in trouble. The shop's closed. You're out of business. Both of you. I see either one of you on the street again, you're going to get serious headaches. Remember the name. Umberto Lugano, a man of respect."

The bag of money had burned almost down to the pavement. The collector couldn't take his eyes off it. Neither could the shark.

BONNIE KEPT HER SEAT and stared at the newspaper she held, as though engrossed. At four in the morning, hardly anyone was in the Continental Trailways Bus Terminal, but the people she wanted to see were there. The two girls had been there for a long time. All night. The woman had been there an hour. Now the woman made her move. Bonnie was close enough to hear.

"Hey. You two live here?"

The two girls looked up at the tall, thin woman whose name Bolan had told Bonnie, was Rose Scalia. She was about forty-five years old, and the makeup with which she tried to conceal her age only served to make her look bizarre—what with arched, plucked eyebrows, blue eye shadow, mascara, rouged cheeks and a heavy application of dark red lipstick. She wore expensive clothes, though—a gray cashmere skirt and jacket, a white silk blouse and jewelry more tasteful than her makeup.

Rose sat down on the bench beside the two girls. "You know what happens next?" she asked.

The girls shook their heads.

The woman glanced around the brightly lighted terminal. "Pretty soon the cops make their morning sweep. They've noticed you two. You're gonna get picked up and taken to the juvenile slammer. End of the trip."

One of the girls was blond, the other a redhead with a freckled complexion. Both of them were pretty. Neither was more than fifteen years old.

"I guess we better get out of here," the redhead said.

"I would, if I were you," Rose Scalia agreed.

"Yeah," the blonde said. "Hassled, hassled, hassled."

"So where'll you go?" Rose asked. She pretended casual interest, only a sociable question, nothing significant.

The redhead shrugged. "They'll hassle us on the street. They already did that."

"You're from out of town?"

They nodded.

"Vermont?"

"Maine," the blonde replied. "Ass end of the world."

Rose smiled and nodded. "Came to the city and—" she chuckled. "Haven't found what you're looking for. So, what is it you're looking for?"

The blonde pulled hard on her cigarette, then tossed it on the floor. "Fun."

"You broke?"

The blonde shook her head. "Not really."

"Well, I guess you'll be getting a bus home, huh?"

"Like hell." The redhead laughed.

Rose smiled. "You're too young to get a job, you know. The law's not very good to girls your age. So, watch out for the cops." She stood, as if to leave. "Uh, I run a little motel."

The blonde smirked. "They warned us about women like you."

Rose smiled. "I bet they did."

The girl's chin rose defiantly. "So, what would we do at your motel? Or should I ask?"

"You're not stupid. What do you think?"

"It's a deal," the redhead replied.

Bonnie followed the three out of the bus terminal. Rose Scalia led the two girls to a BMW. As they left the parking lot, Bonnie turned the key in the ignition and followed in a red Honda.

BOLAN ARRIVED at the motel a little after dawn, chauffeured in the red Honda by Bonnie. When she pulled into the parking lot, the BMW was still parked in front.

The motel was a one-story brick building in a state of disrepair, set in a declining neighborhood. Cans, bottles and rain-soggy trash paper lay scattered among the coarse weeds that bordered the parking lot. What had once been a neon sign saying OFFICE was now only a rusting hulk. Without tubing, it was now readable only by squinting at the stains on the face, where heat from the tubing had burned away the black paint.

The assortment of cars in the parking lot was suggestive—two Mercedes sedans, a Porsche, a Ferrari and a Cadillac. It took no imagination to figure out why these expensive vehicles were parked at this decrepit motel.

Bolan and Bonnie entered the office door. Inside they found just a room with a couple of chairs and a cigarette-scarred table.

"Anybody home?"

After a long moment a hulk of a man—fat, bald, glowering—came out from a room behind the apparent office. "Bug out," he grunted. "Motel's all full."

"I want to see Rose," Bolan demanded.

"You go to hell," the man muttered.

He turned his back, and Bolan grabbed him by the shirt, spun him around, driving one fist into his gut and another into his nose. The hulk dropped to his knees, his nose broken. He shook his head as if to clear it, then he reached into his pocket and drew a .25-caliber automatic.

"Uh-uh," Bonnie said, aiming her Beretta at the middle of his forehead.

"Shit . . ."

Rose appeared in the doorway. "What the hell . . . ?"

Bonnie moved the muzzle of the Beretta so it pointed halfway between the hulk's forehead and Rose's belly. The madam lifted her hands.

"Hey, guys," she soothed, "take it easy. What you want? We got a few bucks. You—"

Bolan's Desert Eagle filled his right hand. He pushed past the dazed hulk, kicking the .25 automatic across the room and far out of his reach, and stepped into the room behind the office.

The two fifteen-year-olds sat naked on a couch. The air of the room was heavy with the distinctive smell of marijuana, but, what was more important, several lines of coke were spread out on the table in front of the couch, and the blonde seemed already to have sniffed a jolt. She looked at Bolan with dreamy eyes, and she lazily tossed a soda straw on the table. The redhead grabbed for her clothes, but the blonde only smiled at Bolan and leaned back in the couch.

"Come in and sit down," he called over his shoulder to Rose and the hulk.

They came in and sat down in two cheap vinyl-covered chairs.

"My girlfriend here," Bolan announced, "has shot two men during the past eight hours. She has no hesitation about pulling the trigger. If either of you two even starts to stand up, she's going to put a slug in your guts. So take it easy. This isn't going to take long."

"You know whose place this is?" Rose asked.

"Yeah," Bolan replied. "That's why we're here."

"You're a dead man, mister."

"Who's going to get the contract?" Bolan asked. "Tony Cipirello, you think?"

"You better hope not."

"No problem. Cipirello got himself whacked."

Rose's jaw dropped, and her eyes widened with fear.

"Now, do as I say," Bolan ordered. "Don't do anything to make my friend nervous."

He walked to the door that opened on the left-side corridor and the doors to ten motel rooms. Holding up the Desert Eagle, the warrior fired a .44 Magnum slug into the ceiling, the roar of the big automatic shaking the building.

"All right, gentlemen!" he yelled. "Everybody up and out! Every man in the office in one minute! If anybody has an idea about going out a window or the back door, forget it. You just might get shot."

Bolan walked across the front of the motel and did the same thing in the other corridor.

Within the specified time frame he had seven men, none of them fully dressed, backed against the wall in the room where Rose and the hulk sat frozen. The girls who had been with them in the rooms wandered in, too—confused, blinking, teary.

"What a pretty little deal," Bolan said. "Teenage girls and middle-aged men. Wait until the news photogs get here and see this!"

"Hey, man! Jesus!"

"I want your driver's licenses, gentlemen, driver's licenses with pictures on them. Toss them on the table there. My lovely assistant will collect them."

"Hey, what are you going to do?"

"I am appointing you gentlemen, honest businessmen all, to a committee for the rehabilitation of these girls. You're all movers and shakers. You can make ways for these girls to get the kind of care they need, to be detoxified, to go home, to get their lives in order. You're going to take responsibility for that. That's how you're going to keep your names out of the news."

Bolan picked up the driver's licenses the men had sullenly thrown onto the table. "Okay. We're going to set up an informal foundation for these kids. Rose is going to put whatever money she has on the premises in the kitty, to get it started. You gentlemen will supplement that with whatever it takes."

Bonnie gestured with the muzzle of the Beretta and led Rose out to get whatever cash she had on hand.

"I haven't introduced myself. My name is Mack Bolan."

"Bolan?" the hulk grunted. "If you'd said that to start with, you wouldn't have had to—" He touched his bloody, broken nose. "I heard the name many times," he added unnecessarily.

"Okay, you're out of business," Bolan said. "Just send the word, you and Rose, to Cesare Frenchi that he's history."

"Bolan..." murmured a heavyset man wearing only his trousers. "I've heard of you for years. Can I talk to you a minute? I mean, so it's only us who can hear?"

Bolan gestured toward a corner of the room.

The heavy man had begun to sweat. He glanced at the others and lowered his voice. "I'm Kozinski," he said, nodding at Bolan's handful of licenses. "I'm a member of the state legislature. I'm finished if this gets out."

"I guess you would be," Bolan responded coldly.

"Okay. A man does what... Anyway, Rose doesn't know who I am. None of the guys do. Except one." He sighed. "I can make this thing work like you say and do something for these kids. Give me a chance, Bolan."

"You got one."

"Thanks. I heard you were in town. So you're taking out Frenchi. He's an animal. I'm on his pad, but I tell you, he's an animal. Okay, listen. Look out for Terranova. He's not your usual hoodlum. In time he'd have killed Frenchi and taken over for himself. Watch out for him."

Bolan looked past Kozinski, at the others. "This gentleman will be your unofficial chairman," he said to them. "Listen to him. He knows I'm serious. I'll be watching what you do. If any of you have any other connections with Cesare Frenchi, you can forget them. Frenchi is history."

THE FAMILY'S BUSINESS wasn't all located on derelict real estate in deteriorating neighborhoods. Or in Cesare Frenchi's house. Salvatore Balestrino had presided over business operations from a handsome old brick building on Beacon Street, with a view of Boston Common. And, though Sally was now in jail, the countinghouse for most of the Frenchi enterprises was still in the Beacon Street house.

The house contained the corporate offices of Caesar Cartage, Salsa Importing, Inc., Frenchi Realty and CF Financial—all Frenchi enterprises, all covers for his real operations. Seven accountants juggled the books and manipulated the tax returns to conceal—to the extent it was possible to conceal—the true sources of the tens of millions of dollars that came in from collectors. The pushers, loan sharks, madams, hijackers, collectors and leg breakers weren't allowed near the corporate offices. In fact, Cesare Frenchi himself rarely went there. He was more at home among his soldiers than among the technocrats who gave his enterprises a semblance of legality and rational management.

He telephoned often, though, on a scrambled telephone line.

"Burned it? Burned the money? He didn't even take it? We're up against crazy men! This is crazy, Ollie. Plus a load of stuff? And Rose's operation! Hey! Does the guy know that we sent a real finger this time?"

"To be honest with you, Cesare," Oliver Piemonte replied, "I hope he doesn't. It's like you say, we're dealing with an unbalanced mind. If he knows you—"

"Finger!" Frenchi screamed. "He's going to get a whole corpse!"

Piemonte picked up his cup and sipped coffee. He would wait out Frenchi's tantrum, as he had done many times before. While Frenchi raved on the telephone, Piemonte drank coffee and gazed idly at a computer screen covered with numbers.

"We have a serious problem, Cesare," he said when he could get a word in. "Believe it or not, we're running short on cash."

"Because a lunatic burned up a laundry bag? Because of what we lost the night Bolan killed Henry? Because—"

"Because business has started to dry up," Piemonte said. "Hal Harvard last night took one look at this fellow Lugano and scrammed. We didn't just lose the money, but we also lost the collector. Cipirello's two soldiers were so scared by Bolan that they lammed. This morning Bolan and Lugano hit a book. It won't open again. The guys are afraid to open it. Guys have been skimming, of course. They've all got money. They're lying low until Bolan's gone."

"How 'bout you, Oliver. You buggin' out?"

"I haven't yet," Piemonte replied with calm contempt.

"Yeah, well you better not. Cesare Frenchi has a long memory. Tell those guys. Cesare Frenchi has a long memory."

"So does Bolan, I'd judge."

"Ollie . . . Ollie, I want a couple hundred thou."

"I don't know where you are, Cesare."

"Yeah. Well, I'm going to leave it that way. For now. You might get a visit from Bolan yourself, and you just might have a big mouth."

BOLAN VISITED Piemonte about noon, accompanied by Umberto Lugano and Bonnie. Piemonte recognized Bonnie from the times he had seen her at the house—Cesare's plaything, now grim and carrying a gun.

"It's all in our heads," Piemonte explained to Bolan. "That's the way it has to be. It's in Salvatore Balestrino's head, and mine, and in the heads of two or three other men who work here. But nothing on paper."

"Not in Frenchi's head?" Bolan asked skeptically.

"Frenchi has his talents. A head for numbers isn't one of them."

Bolan and his companions had been able to walk into the building without firing a shot, without even using muscle. Thanks to Balestrino, who had sent an order from his jail cell that the hardmen were to be pulled out and Ollie Piemonte was to talk to Bolan. Why? Because Sally had surrendered. He faced a certain life sentence with no chance of parole, no possibility of ever seeing the outside again, unless he cooperated one hundred percent.

The way he figured, Sally had told Ollie, the Frenchi Family just might be dead. Guys like them—Sally and Ollie—had better get out with what they could, while they could. Ollie had talked to Balestrino before he talked to Cesare. It had made him bolder in his conversation with his capo. The fact was, he *was* pulling out.

"I have a tape recorder here," Bolan said. "I want the whole deal laid out on tape. Everything."

"What'll you do if I don't?" Piemonte asked.

"Guess."

"Yes," Piemonte said coolly. "You have a reputation."

"But first I want to know where Janice Elliott is. And where Frenchi is."

"I can tell you they're together," Piemonte replied. "Where?" He shrugged. "I don't know. You can't find out from me, because I don't know. He even asked me to send him money this morning, then dropped it because he'd rather not have the money than have to tell me where he is."

"I have to believe him," Bolan said to Lugano.

Lug nodded. He knew the ways of these people, and he too believed Piemonte.

"So talk." Bolan placed the tape recorder on Piemonte's desk. "For the FBI and the IRS, for the Massachusetts State Police, for the city police. Talk."

"What's in it for me?"

"What's in it for you if you don't?" Bolan countered. "That's the question."

"I can talk and talk," Piemonte told him. "You won't be able to tell if I've told you anything worthwhile or not. It's complicated. It will take months to figure out."

"Supposing I believe you one way or the other," Bolan queried, "just what do you have in mind?"

Piemonte lifted his chin high. The corners of his mouth were turned down. "I'll talk for an hour or so, then I want you to take me out of this building and let me get into a cab. I want an hour's start."

"Who are you running from?"

Piemonte's solemn face softened for an instant with a hint of a smile. "You," he replied. "Frenchi. The FBI, the IRS, the Massachusetts State Police. Who else?"

"You won't get far," Lugano stated.

"I'll have had my try."

12

"Your brother is a madman," Giuseppe Rossi announced. "It's the plain truth, Vinnie."

Vinnie Frenchi took no apparent offense at what Rossi had just said. He sat in Rossi's Manhattan office, his hands clasped firmly on the conference-room table. Except for the ostentatious diamond-encrusted heavy gold ring on his left hand, he looked much like Rossi—a clean-lined, square-jawed, gray-haired man, conservatively dressed. His gray suit was as well tailored as Rossi's. His calm, quiet voice sounded like Rossi's. He was deeply tanned, though, which Rossi wasn't. Vinnie Frenchi spent much time at poolside in Los Angeles, where he was *consigliere* to Don Gaspare Nicolosi.

"What Joe says is true," said Bill O'Neill, the Irish mob leader who shared Boston with the Frenchi Family. "Cesare is... Well, how do you say?"

"Unbalanced," Vinnie Frenchi said calmly. "Who knows better than I? But Cesare isn't your problem. Not for the moment. Let me suggest, gentlemen, that you have let my brother's aberrant conduct blind your eyes to what's happening in Boston."

The members of the Commission glared coldly at this upstart *consigliere* from Los Angeles, come—as they supposed—to defend his brother. Sestola was there, as well as Ferraro from Philadelphia, DeMaioribus from Providence, Lugesi from Cleveland, Benvenuto from Detroit and Basilio from Chicago.

Vinnie Frenchi continued. "You can do what you want about my brother. I don't care. Later, you can give his businesses to Bill O'Neill, or to somebody else you choose—I'm not here to argue about that. I'm here to recall to your minds a bit of history, the history of what this man Bolan has done to some of us. Who better to remind you than a son of Sergio Frenchi?"

"Vinnie's got special qualifications," DeMaioribus grunted.

"Do you understand what Bolan has done?" Vinnie Frenchi asked. "In a week, he's almost dried up revenues in Boston. My brother called me in L.A. to ask for a loan from Don Gaspare, to pay off some crack manufacturer he owes a bundle to. My brother is short of money! And you, Bill. Are you going to tell us that Bolan's campaign against the Frenchis hasn't hurt *your* businesses?"

Bill O'Neill nodded thoughtfully. "Collections are off," he acknowledged. "The sharks are all but off the streets. Dealers are scared. Collectors are scared. Yeah, Vinnie, you got a point. It's not just Cesare who's hurting."

Vinnie Frenchi glanced at each man, nodding. "Right. This month, Boston. Who's to say he won't move to Providence next, or Philly, or... Well, wherever. What he's doing to the Frenchi Family now he could be doing to the Rossi Family next week."

"Not exactly," Rossi said. "We don't operate the same way."

"No? Well, let me ask you this. What if next Tuesday Bolan walks into these offices and puts a slug through your forehead, Joe? How you operate is not the point. It's how *Bolan* operates that counts. If he decides to give you a headache, you get a headache. He's called the Executioner, don't forget."

"So, what are you talking about?" Rossi asked. "You want to put out a million-dollar contract? It's been done before."

"'Contract,'" Frenchi sneered. "Frankly, gentlemen, a contract is the way we avoid responsibility when hard and dirty work has to be done. Send some ambitious, greedy and not-too-bright wise guy to make a hit. We don't have to see the blood."

"I've seen plenty of blood in my day," Al Ferraro growled.

"Right, Al," Frenchi conceded respectfully. "You've done the muscle work and the brain work, both. So what's *your* judgment? You see my point? What do you think?"

Rossi watched Vinnie Frenchi recruit an ally, and there was nothing he could do to stop him. *This* Frenchi was shrewd. Why hadn't he become head of the Family? He was older, smarter. The Bolan problem wouldn't have come back if Vinnie Frenchi had been in charge in Boston.

Of course, there was an explanation. He was too cautious. Cesare was a wild man. He was also ruthless, vicious. Very likely he would have killed Vinnie. Vinnie had distanced himself from Cesare rather than fight him and had survived. Now he would survive again, because there was no doubt that Cesare was a dead man, whether Bolan took him out or a hitter from the Commission did it.

"It is my judgment," Ferraro said in the measured speech he often liked to affect, supposing it was the way the old Sicilians had talked, "that this man Bolan is the greatest threat we face. While some of us have changed our ways, like the Rossi Family has, Bolan still fights the old way, like we were Capone or Luciano. Anyway, like Vinnie says, he can shut a town down anytime he gets mad. I say we should make the elimination of this Executioner Bolan our first job. We are none of us safe while he lives.''

"Okay," DeMaioribus said. "So who does it?"

"No headhunter," Vinnie Frenchi warned. "No single headhunter could handle it. What we need is an army.''

"Will Don Gaspare send somebody?" Rossi asked.

Frenchi nodded. "Don Gaspare has sent two hitters with me. That's his contribution—two.''

"I too will provide the services of two men," Ferraro offered.

"Me, too," DeMaioribus grunted.

"That's six," Frenchi said. He looked at Lugesi and Benvenuto.

They nodded.

"All right," Rossi said. "I have a specialist I can assign to the job. A woman. She's very good at her work. But it's not enough just to send a dozen headhunters to Boston. We have to plan the job, coordinate. A dozen hitters working independently will just get themselves killed by Bolan. We need pictures of the man. Most of our people wouldn't know him if they saw him. We need—''

"I'm carrying a picture," Frenchi interrupted. "Also, one of my men ran up against Bolan a few years ago. He survived, and he can tell our other people how the man operates.''

"He's got Lug Lugano working with him," Sestola said.

"And a woman," O'Neill added.

"Who is the woman?" Frenchi queried.

"We don't know, but I know how we can find out," Rossi responded.

"Can you get word to your brother?" Sestola asked Frenchi.

"Yes."

"Well, tell him to lay off those two women he's holding. We sent that word once before, and he told us to go to hell. Tell him we'll handle Bolan for him, but if he messes around any more with those two women he's gonna have a serious headache."

"I've told him that already."

"Tell him again."

"And I think it would be a good idea if you tell us where he is, Vinnie," Rossi suggested.

"He's on Block Island," Vinnie Frenchi told them.

No one ever suspected her until it was too late. She was the most successful headhunter he had ever employed, and Giuseppe Rossi held her in a degree of awe.

Salina Beaudreau was six foot two, a black woman of extraordinarily exotic appearance. It was strange to call her black, actually, because her skin was a smooth golden brown. She wore her hair no more than a half an inch long—indeed less, and he had seen her with her head shaved. She wore dark red lipstick and eye shadow of a violet hue. This morning she was dressed in a black leather miniskirt and a silk blouse of the same violet color as her eye shadow. She also wore a half dozen gold chains around her neck.

Rossi doubted she rode the subway wearing that much gold. It would be dangerous. People had been killed for the gold chains that were so much in style among teenagers making money from dealing in crack.

He smiled to himself. No, Salina Beaudreau didn't ride the subways. She handled no more than two jobs a year, but she was never paid less than half a million dollars. Anyway, a subway punk who tried to jerk the chains from around *her* neck would likely find himself coughing blood and wondering where the slugs in his lungs had come from.

"It's worth a million," she said calmly when he told her who she was to hit. She shrugged lightly, and a little smile flitted across her face. "Two million."

Rossi nodded. "One million is the fee. Two million...? I don't know. You do the job, and I'll put out the word that we ought to pay you another million."

"This job is my retirement." She took a pack of cigarettes from her purse and tapped out a long, thin cigarette. She lit it with a tiny lighter. "One way or the other. The man won't kill easy. There's a big risk he'll get *me*. Y' know?"

"Salina," Rossi said, "I think the job is worth two million. I have one million authorized. If you succeed, I will *try* to get you the second million. I don't want you to think I've promised it. I will *try*. Understood?"

She nodded.

He always made sure the woman understood the deal. If there had been any misunderstanding, it was not inconceivable she could go after him.

"Anyway," he said, lifting an attaché case from under his desk. "Here's half a million in advance." He glanced at his watch. "Would you like to have lunch?"

She glanced at *her* watch. "I can still catch the noon shuttle for Boston. The picture and all are in the briefcase with the money?"

"Right."

"Okay," she said. "We got a deal. If I survive, I'll be back for my second half-million—or the million and a half, if you can get it. I remind you, I'm worth it."

Rossi nodded. "Every nickel."

"Wish me luck."

"I do," he said sincerely.

Salina rose. "Okay. If we'd gone to lunch we'd have raised a glass to it. Instead . . . a fist. To the death of Mack

Bolan! I'll take that son of a bitch out, or I won't be back."

SALINA BEAUDREAU CHECKED IN at the Parker House. Once in her room overlooking the State House, she unpacked her tools of the trade—Brownings.

Salina took a shower, luxuriating for a long time in the hot water and steam; even though it was a warm day, she enjoyed letting the hot water stream over her, relaxing her muscles.

She knew she was an exotic woman. All kinds of men, black and white, yearned for her. Some had died yearning for her. She was scornful of that. What they had to offer—she could take it or leave it. What she had to offer—they couldn't; they had to have it. She wondered about Mack Bolan.

Too bad about him. Too bad things were the way they were. A woman like her and a man like him . . . Well, they would make a pair, wouldn't they? In a way, they weren't so different.

Wasn't he full of bitterness for what the world had done to people he cared for? Hadn't he identified his enemies and gone after them? Didn't he put aside the niceties and do his job, whatever that meant?

She wished she could have met him some other way.

THE BIG ITALIAN WASN'T so difficult; everybody knew him. Everybody knew Bolan, too, but in a different way. They knew his name. A few even knew his face. He moved everywhere, but he managed to remain inconspicuous. Not Lugano. The Big Lug made a splash. In fact, he loved to make a splash. That was his thing.

Besides, after years in stir he was horny. And thirsty. He was making his way around in Boston. Bolan probably tried to keep him quiet, but it couldn't be easy. Not with a man like Umberto Lugano.

O'Neill had sent the word that Lugano had been seen around town. There were several places where he might be found.

Shamrock. How many bars in Boston were called Shamrock? How many were full of half-literate Irish thugs? She had plenty of experience with the type.

The first two bars weren't the right Shamrock. Wearing tight shorts, showing sensual bare legs, long, muscular and brown, she generated exactly the response she intended in those two bars. She was accosted, propositioned... crudely, in sexist, racist terms. She fended off overweight, beer-filled hoodlums, one after another.

Then in the third...

"Lug been in?" she asked the bartender.

"Lug...?"

"Lug Lugano," she snapped. "He asked me to meet him in this dump. Been in or not?"

"Who the hell you think you are, nigger?"

Salina reached lazily for a mug of beer in front of a man to her right. She dashed the beer in the bartender's face, right to left, then came back across, left to right, with the empty mug, catching him alongside the ear. Blood flowed from a gash in his neck.

"Watch who you call nigger, honky," she gritted. "Now, answer the question. Lug been in?"

The bartender ducked under the bar and came up with a baseball bat. But when he turned and confronted her, he found himself staring into the muzzle of a Browning.

The customers edged back.

"I only asked a simple question. Has Lug been in?"

The bartender dropped the bat and staggered back against the rack behind the bar, raising his hands before him as if he were being held up.

"Hey, lady," he said. "I don't know no Lug."

Salina smiled as she put the Browning back into her soft leather purse. "Well, why didn't you say so?" she asked sweetly.

BILL O'NEILL'S ASSESSMENT of Lug Lugano was accurate. After eight years in prison, Lug was horny and thirsty. He'd taken an interest at first in Bonnie Hennings. In fact, he had taken her to bed. But she was reluctant to give him all he wanted, and Lug was determined to make up for lost time.

He didn't have time for a girl who was looking for a different life. He wasn't in the position to give her one. Life was short and it was dangerous. He was on the street now, but in a month he might be back in stir, or dead. He had a commitment, Bolan had said, but commitments had been welshed on before and could be again.

Boston wasn't a bad town for him. He hadn't worked here much. Guys weren't after him. Except maybe the Frenchis, and they didn't know him and were on the run anyway. It was damned good the way Bolan had knocked the Frenchi Family on its ear. Lug had enjoyed working with Bolan. It was as sure as hell better to work *with* the Executioner than to work against him.

Bolan and the girl were out somewhere. Lug hadn't quite figured it out, Bolan and Bonnie. Maybe there was something going on there. If so, the girl had better be careful. Bolan was no more likely to offer a woman a commitment than Lug was.

Anyway, they were out. The Frenchis had better worry about where. For himself, he'd take the couple or three hours they had left him alone to indulge himself a little.

Bolan had provided money. Lug wasn't rich, but he had enough in his pockets to do what he had in mind.

The Shamrock. Usually there were a few good-looking chicks hanging around, and if he wasn't good-looking enough himself to attract them without paying, then he would pay them. That was okay, too. When you did it for pay, nobody suggested any obligation. The man would go his way, the woman hers. A nice clean way to have it.

A lot of guys wanted to give him a headache over his working for Bolan. A lot of guys. Some of them were dead already. Having watched Bolan operate, he knew a lot more about the guy. It was too late for him, Lug, to switch sides permanently. Sooner or later, he'd have to go back to the life. What else was there for a man like him?

The wise guys would have to let him come back. He was a made man. *He* wasn't a traitor. He was helping Bolan kill a traitor. The Commission knew that.

Or maybe... He was tired. He'd seen too much. He wondered what the Feds would offer a man who'd come over.

Squalor. That's what they'd offer. The company of guys who thought playing bridge was a big deal. The federal witness protection program. What about Vegas? Atlantic City? Action? Hell, they didn't know how to appreciate it themselves, so how could they know how much it meant to a man?

Lug had left his necktie off this evening. He wore a dark blue pin-striped suit and a white shirt. In its harness under his suit jacket he carried the Beretta 93-R that Bolan thought was such a great gun. It was, actually. He had a couple hundred in his wallet. He should be able to find some fun. If he couldn't, he'd use the Beretta to increase his bankroll.

How would Bolan like that?

First the Shamrock, a beer or two, then… Well, if there wasn't any great action at the Sham, then maybe a good Italian dinner. God, he loved Italian food!

They didn't know him yet, not really. He'd been in twice. It wasn't a good idea to get known too well in any one bar. The Shamrock was okay. The interesting thing was, the place wasn't dominated by Irish. Odd neighborhood. He liked it. Irish, sure, but also Italians, French, Poles, all kinds.

As Lug walked through the door he caught sight of a tall, gorgeous woman standing at the bar. Six feet of coffee-and-cream perfection, she seemed to be everything he was looking for.

Could a man have this kind of incredible luck? he thought.

Lug took a place at the bar beside her and ordered a beer.

"Hi," he said.

She looked down at him and nodded. "Hello."

"By yourself?" he asked.

She shrugged.

"Uh, well. Can I buy you a drink?"

She looked down at him again and shrugged. "Why do you want to buy me a drink?"

Lug grinned. "Friendship."

"We're not friends."

"Could be. Couldn't we?"

"Why?" she asked coolly.

"Well, why kid around?"

At long last she smiled. "Figured," she murmured.

"Straight talk, huh?" Lug said. "I'm a lonely guy. I got two hundred on me, that's all. How about an Italian dinner, with a nice red wine, and then— Well, then . . . you know. Interested?"

She stared at him as if she were making a careful judgment. She'd come in here in those shorts, showing those legs, and in that blouse, barely hiding those breasts—and she was staring as if she were assessing him. She had class.

"Name's Sally," she said.

"They call me Lug. Is it okay, then?"

"A real, first-class dinner. Balance of the two hundred to me."

He nodded.

"I'm sort of paying for this dinner, you might say. Something good, Lug. Not just your damned spaghetti. Veal. Chianti."

He grinned. "You're talkin' my language."

Lug put some money on the bar to pay for the beer he hadn't drunk. As he led "Sally" out of the bar, he saw the smirks of the other patrons, and he flashed them a triumphant grin and wink.

"We need a cab," he said. "You can't get good Italian food in this neighborhood. Then we'll go to my motel. Okay?"

"Okay. Cab's not so easy to get around here."

"Couple of blocks. Cabs cruise the Main street down there."

Lug put his arm through hers, thinking about how lucky he was. He'd never been with a girl like this one. It was going to be an adventure like . . . He'd ask Bolan for another loan and take her out again tomorrow night. Maybe—

As they walked along the dark street, Salina reached into her purse. Lug looked up at the moon, and suddenly he felt a sharp pain in his side, under his armpit. Then another one. He realized what had happened as he slid to the ground. He'd been hit.

13

"It's getting rough," DiRosario said.

Bolan nodded. "It's always rough, and there's no end to how rough it can get. Are you talking about backing away?"

DiRosario shook his head. He'd brought the news of Lug Lugano's death.

Bolan had already suspected it. Whatever else Lug had been, he'd been faithful to his appointments. When he didn't show at the arranged time, Bolan was ready to accept the worst.

"It was clean," DiRosario said. "Clean and cool. Three .25-caliber slugs through his armpit and into his lungs and heart. Professional."

"Baby Browning?" Bolan asked.

DiRosario nodded. "In the hands of a pro. Ballistics matches the slugs to one found in three priors. Whoever the hitter is, he's taken out two federal witnesses and a Mafia don. No description. No idea who he is."

"Nothing?"

"The angles suggest a man over six feet tall. The little Browning is quiet, easily concealed."

"Doesn't even need a silencer." Bolan shook his head. "Where did it happen?"

"A street in Southie. Do you know what Lugano was doing there?"

"Cruising," Bolan replied. "Looking for fun, the same as any man would be who'd spent eight years in the pen. What do the police have?"

DiRosario shook his head. "Not much."

"Do they care?"

"I can't say they do care, much. As far as they're concerned, he—"

"As far as they're concerned," Bolan interrupted, "Lug was an Italian ex-con, likely to get hit, and nobody gives a damn if he was."

"Well, I wouldn't go that far."

"How many men do they have on it?"

"I don't know."

"How many men do *you* have on it?"

DiRosario sighed. "None. I can't. It's not under federal jurisdiction."

"No. Of course not. I want the address."

LUG HAD BEEN KILLED while walking on the street. He wouldn't have walked far—he'd have caught a cab if he'd had any great distance to travel. Therefore, he was killed while on his way from somewhere to somewhere, and one of those somewheres wasn't very far from the place where he was gunned down and left bleeding to death on the sidewalk. The fact whirled around in Bolan's head.

A thousand possibilities? No, not more than half a dozen. The neighborhood wasn't part of Lug's old stomping ground. It was unlikely that he was going anywhere except a public place—a bar. And knowing Lug, one where he would have tried to pick up a hooker.

Bolan walked the streets that evening; checking out the bars, one after another.

Irish bars, most of them, serving beer chiefly, where burly, flushed men drank standing and shifted their attention back and forth from conversation to the above-bar television set that seemed to dominate all these places. Neighborhood clubs. Family bars where hookers would have been identified and shoved out, pronto. Not the kind of places where Lug Lugano, hurting in all his manly desires, would look for relief.

But then Bolan walked into the Shamrock. There must have been a hundred Boston beer-joints called the Shamrock, and this one much like the other Shamrocks, but not much like the other bars in the neighborhood. A little rougher. Not the kind of place where an Irish truck driver would bring his wife while he was home between trips. Nor the kind of place where his wife would bring their daughter for a couple of beers during the evenings while the truck driver was away. Something subtle in the atmosphere, something not the same.

Yet not very different. But here, if Bolan judged right, a hooker wouldn't be shoved out the door just because she came in and asked for a beer. Somewhere they had a game going—maybe in back, maybe upstairs. Looking around, Bolan guessed you could find a loan shark in the crowd, and just maybe, if you asked right, you could find someone who'd sell you a sniff or a shot.

Bill O'Neill's territory, one of the few places left in the country where an Irish mob was in control.

Bolan walked to the bar and asked for a beer.

The bartender sized him up as he drew the draft, his eyes unfriendly. He might not shove a hooker out the door, but he obviously didn't like new customers—not at first anyway, not until he'd had a chance to take their measure.

"I'm looking for a guy," Bolan said as the bartender slammed the glass of beer down on the counter.

"Aren't we all?"

"Big Italian," Bolan continued. "Broken nose, scars, tough."

The bartender shrugged and started to walk away.

Bolan reached out and caught him by the arm. "Tell you what, my friend," he said quietly. "I have a rule. Guys don't walk away from me when I'm talking to them. You know?"

The bartender jerked his arm away and, for a moment glared angrily at Bolan. Then he exhaled, frowned and turned thoughtful. Maybe he guessed the identity of the man in the Red Sox jacket. Maybe he'd never seen such concentrated force and anger in a man's eyes. Whatever . . . he decided not to walk away from this man.

"You're talkin' about the guy who got killed." He jerked his thumb toward the door and the street.

"Okay," Bolan admitted. "Right. Even so, I was supposed to meet him. Who'd he meet here? Who'd he leave with?"

"The cops already asked," the bartender replied. "I told 'em."

"Tell me."

The bartender glanced around, obviously uncomfortable with being seen talking to a stranger who was asking significant questions. Still, he judged it wasn't a good idea to tell this guy to buzz off.

"I told the cops," he said quietly. "The guy left here with a black hooker. Six feet tall. Gorgeous. She'd never been in here before. He had, two or three times. They left together. The guy paid for a beer and didn't drink it. She set him up, I got no doubt. He thought he was goin' out for a fun time. She led him to— Well, you know."

"Anybody follow them?"

The bartender shook his head. "Hell, man. When she was standin' at the bar, I was looking at her front side.

When she was leavin', I was staring at her back side. I was lookin' at *her*. J. Edgar Hoover could've been following them, I wouldn't have noticed."

"Describe this woman a little more."

"BE DAMNED" Italo Minozzo muttered. "It's *him*."

The woman sitting beside him in a booth, eight feet from where Bolan stood at the bar, nodded. Her name was Vittoria Gimignano. Minozzo was better known as Tally Man, she was Vicky Jim. They had worked together for years. He was the hitter; she was his bait.

The unhappy truth was that Vicky had worked with Tally so long that she was no longer of much value as bait. She was almost fifty years old, and the attractions that had made her bait had faded. Still, she was knowledgeable and had an instinct for the hunt and the kill that Tally appreciated. Over the years they had set up and hit more than fifty men and six women. Neither of them had ever been arrested, neither identified or suspected, neither hurt.

They worked for Don Gaspare Nicolosi and had been sent to Boston at the request of Vinnie Frenchi.

They were strangers in the Shamrock as much as Bolan was, and they had been welcomed with as much enthusiasm as he had—that is to say, with none. Tally, who was sixty years old, carried his years badly. He was bald, wore bifocal glasses, and he sagged in their booth, his shoulders rounded as he hunched over his beer. His gray, summer-weight sport jacket was shabby. The regulars in the bar looked on him with contempt, never guessing—even remotely—that the old man they scorned had killed fifty-six people.

Vicky was taller than Tally and sat with a straighter posture. She was a bleached blonde, with her hair piled on top of her head. Her face bore the marks of the plastic surgery that had corrected her wrinkles and sagging eyes and jowls. Her makeup was heavy and shiny, her eyebrows plucked into thin arches. She wore a white silk blouse and skintight black slacks.

Tally and Vicky weren't husband and wife and had never been lovers. In fact, they saw each other only when they were working. Tally spent his time in Las Vegas, where he lived in a motel and divided his time between the casinos and the private games. Vicky lived in a modest beach house at Malibu. She received only ten percent of his fees, but on that money she lived a comfortable life with a succession of men who shared her house. Once, at her request, Tally had rid her of one of them.

Vicky nodded. "The Executioner."

"Doesn't look difficult, does it?"

"A hell of a lot more difficult than it looks," she said, nodding ironically.

"Smart work..." Tally mused. "The other operator, whoever he was, took out Lugano last night. Bolan was bound to show, they said, and here he is."

"Too many people know what's up, Tally."

He nodded agreement. "The first time I ever saw two Families cooperate on one hit. 'Coordinated.' That's the word Vinnie used, coordinated. Like military strategy, he said."

Vicky shrugged. "Well, there he is. I've heard of him for more years than I want to admit. Damn tough way to set him up—taking out another guy to—"

"Lugano had to go," Tally interrupted. "Sooner or later."

"I suppose so. So what do we do now?"

"Sit still," he said. "I want to check."

He meant he wanted to check his weapon. Over the years Tally had used a variety of pistols, but lately he had developed an affection for a new one—a Charter Arms Bull-dog Pug, a snub-nose, round-grip .44 Special. The Pug delivered one hell of a wallop. It blasted men off their feet, and they never fired back. The big slug scrambled their insides thoroughly, and only once had he had to fire more than one shot. Besides, the Pug went off with a horren-dous roar that terrified every bystander within fifty yards.

Times past, he had sometimes used little silenced pis-tols. Sometimes he'd had to fire three or four times, and the guy had yelled and struggled and pulled his own gun. And civilians had once even got it in their heads to try to stop him.

Not when he fired the Pug. People went for the floor when they heard *that* explosion.

It carried nicely, too, in a hip holster, out of sight under his coat. He really liked that little biscuit. This one was finished in stainless steel. It was a businesslike tool.

"Okay," Tally said. He shoved the Pug back into its holster. "You go out. Follow him. If he gets in a car, get the number. I'll come out a little later, like you and I aren't together. I don't want to take him here. I want to see where he lives. We're supposed to get the woman, too, if we can."

BOLAN'S MOTEL in Watertown was called Quiet Rest, which sounded, Bonnie said, altogether too much like a funeral parlor or cemetery. With Lug gone, he had moved her there. She'd be damned if she'd sleep in a separate room, she said; she'd stay in his room even if she had to sleep on the floor.

"A black woman," she said. "Whatever. Whoever killed Lug, we still have to eat. I've waited for you."

Bolan nodded. "Okay. We'll pick up some burgers."

"What the hell, is the expense account running short? Okay, you don't feel like... Burgers it is."

They left Quiet Rest about 11:15, drove to a fast-food restaurant and were back by 11:45.

Like all motels of its kind, Quiet Rest was dominated by its parking lot, an expanse of cracked asphalt. Tonight a dozen cars were parked outside, indicating that most of the rooms were occupied. Others would be used temporarily during the night. Floodlights mounted on the motel's roof cast their glow into the lot, but two of the four lights were out.

Bolan pulled the rented car into a space toward the front of the motel, near his room. He grabbed the food and left the car on the driver's side, then started around the car to open the passenger door for Bonnie. She had already gotten out and walked around the rear.

A car door slammed toward the back of the parking lot. They saw a woman walk across the back of the lot toward the rear entrance to the motel but paid little attention to her until suddenly she dropped to her knees.

"Hey," Bolan grunted. He handed Bonnie the bag of food and jogged toward the woman.

She was a blonde, older woman, dressed in a white blouse and black slacks, and as he reached her, she sprawled forward with a groan and lay facedown on the pavement.

Bolan knelt beside her. "Ma'am—"

He heard a sharp pop, then instantly the explosion of a big handgun. The warrior threw himself down, rolled over and came up with his Beretta in hand.

A second explosion. He saw the muzzle-flash and heard the slug hit the asphalt.

Bonnie was on her knees, Beretta extended in both hands.

The muzzle-flash had come from between two cars, a Buick and a Ford. Bolan couldn't see anyone crouched there but he fired a 3-round burst into shadows anyway.

The woman beside him was up and running hard toward the door of the motel.

Okay. She'd been a decoy.

Bolan rolled along the pavement, spoiling the aim of the unseen gunman. He scrambled to his feet and dashed toward the corner of the motel, as though in pursuit of the woman. He heard another explosion, and a heavy slug punched into the concrete-block wall just behind him, shattering a block and spraying fragments. He ducked around the corner of the building and put his head out cautiously, looking back.

Bonnie was working her way along the front of the line of parked cars in a low crouch, pressing her body against each car for cover. She'd seen the situation develop before Bolan had. It had been her shot that had ruined the aim of the gunman's first shot. Bolan understood, and now he owed her a similar favor. He gestured at her to stay back.

It looked as if the gunman was trapped between the Buick and the Ford—aware, for sure, that he was fighting two people, each one armed and capable of taking him out. His advantage was in the big-bore gun he was firing, which he had undoubtedly reloaded by now. A slug from that weapon would knock a person sprawling, even from a shot that hit only an arm or leg.

The woman apparently didn't have a weapon. Bolan checked behind him, but he couldn't spot her.

He took a moment to pull the magazine from his Beretta and shove in a fully loaded one, even though he had shots left in the original clip. He hoped Bonnie had remembered to do the same.

He fired another 3-round burst into the shadows between the two cars and heard his bullets ricochet off the fenders and doors. He sprinted across the asphalt to the line of parked cars, taking up a station similar to Bonnie's, only at the other end.

The gunman didn't fire, and Bolan wondered whether the guy had been hit.

He could see Bonnie, two cars over from where they had seen the gunman's muzzle-flashes. She peered over the rear deck of a Pontiac, searching for the man. Bolan waved to her and she nodded.

If she'd stay where she was, preventing the gunman from breaking out into the open parking lot, then Bolan could work his way down the line of cars and find the man.

The warrior lay down on the ground and peered beneath the vehicles, thinking that he might be able to see the gunman's legs. He couldn't; it was too dark. He stood, circled around the hood of an Oldsmobile, and slipped into the narrow space between the Olds and a Volkswagen.

He was two cars from the Buick, and Bonnie was two from the Ford. He waved to her again, hoping she would understand his signal to stay in place. He hoped she understood the peril she was in. They were facing a hit man, an expert. There would be no such thing as a minor wound if he got a good shot at either of them.

Bolan wished he had his own big gun. The Desert Eagle was a match for whatever that cannon was, and he judged it was more accurate, at least in his hands, since the hit man had missed him three times.

He began to edge his way around the nose of the Volkswagen.

"Help! Help! My husband! They're trying to kill my husband!"

The woman, the decoy, staggered into the parking lot, screaming. Half a dozen men, who had crowded behind the doors inside the motel, attracted by the firing in the parking lot, edged cautiously through the doors.

"Hey, lady, come back! The cops—"

"Too late! They've killed my husband," the woman shrieked, and she staggered across the lot toward the Buick and Ford.

Bonnie stood. "Get back!"

For a brief moment she was exposed to the hit man. It was enough. The big pistol roared, and Bonnie was lifted off her feet and thrown to the asphalt, her chest blown open.

The shot hadn't come from between the Buick and the Ford. The hit man had quietly opened the doors of the Buick and crawled through.

Bolan leaped to the roof of the nearest vehicle, vaulted across the roof of the Ford, then to the roof of the Buick. The hit man, small and bald, moved the muzzle of his stubby revolver toward Bolan, but he wasn't fast enough. Bolan had the Beretta set to fire bursts, and three slugs tore through the man's throat, scattering flesh and fragments of his spine.

As the hit man fell back, he yanked convulsively on his trigger, and a futile shot from his .44 revolver exploded toward the sky.

THERE WAS NO POINT in checking Bonnie for vital signs. The big slug had blown her apart. She lay in a spreading, gleaming pool of blood, a twisted corpse sprawled in a posture no living body could ever assume.

The decoy woman had run inside the motel, still screaming. There was no point in chasing her down.

Bolan had left almost nothing in the room. His other weapons were in the car. With a lingering glance at Bonnie, he trotted to his rented car and got out of there.

14

"You want to know who he was?" Hal Brognola asked.

They were in the government Lear jet thirty-eight thousand feet above Pennsylvania, on their way to Washington. Brognola had insisted that Bolan get out of Boston, at least for a day or two—first because he was exhausted, and second because it was obvious that a million-dollar contract was out on him and he needed to rest and reorganize.

Bolan slumped in the seat, idly watching the green countryside below. It was true that he was exhausted, but his exhaustion was of the mind and spirit, not of the body; he'd been more weary than this, many times, and had functioned. His exhaustion was from the double-punch loss of Bonnie and Lug. Not only had he lost them, but he had to acknowledge that someone had acted shrewdly and effectively in locating them and taking them out. The hit last night had been meant for him, of course, and had almost succeeded. If not for Bonnie...

Hanging back as he had raced to help the decoy, Bonnie had spotted the hit man taking aim from the shadows, and she had fired quickly enough to distract him. She had saved Bolan's life.

And lost her own.

"He was Italo Minozzo," Brognola said, "a longtime hit man. A real pro. The slug that killed Bonnie Hennings was matched by the FBI ballistics lab to the slug that killed Joe Ancona."

"Joe Ancona . . . ?"

"He'd have been an important federal witness if he'd lived a little longer. He'd just made his first contacts with the FBI office in Dallas, and then—Italo Minozzo, known as Tally Man. The woman, incidentally, disappeared."

"The decoy."

"Right. She got away clean. We have no idea who she was. In the confusion she got to the car Minozzo had been driving, and before anybody knew what was happening, she took off. So we didn't even get the car, or her fingerprints."

"She was a pro herself."

"I'd like to know how they found you," Brognola said. "How do you suppose they knew you were in that motel?"

Bolan shrugged.

"All right." He squared his shoulders, and his voice hardened to a more businesslike tone. "I'm going to tell you something about Tally Man Minozzo. You've got to cool it on this. Don't get excited about it. Minozzo worked for Don Gaspare Nicolosi."

"Los Angeles."

"Right. And do you know who's Don Gaspare's *consigliere*?"

Bolan frowned, searching his memory. "Vinnie Frenchi."

Brognola nodded. "You got it."

"That explains a thing or two, doesn't it?"

"Let *me* explain something," Brognola said. "You must not go after Vinnie. If something happened to Vinnie, it could be the final straw for Cesare, the straw that would make him kill Janice and Brenda. You've got to leave Vinnie alone."

"Who's idea is that?" Bolan asked.

"I've got orders from the President," Brognola replied. "He and the attorney general discussed it this morning."

"Everybody's been busy," Bolan said dryly. "In twelve hours the FBI does a ballistics check, a print check and identifies Tally Minozzo. The President and the attorney general meet on the case, and you come to Boston and talk me into flying out of town."

"The story is out that Janice and Brenda Elliott have been kidnapped," Brognola said. "We held it as long as we could, but it's out. The *Washington Post* has it this morning. So does the *New York Times*. From this point, it's not a matter of what you want to do or I want to do."

"So, what's the President going to do? Negotiate with Cesare Frenchi?"

"We're going to try to get in touch with him." Brognola sighed. "I'm sorry, big guy, but those are my orders."

"So, what are you going to offer him in return for the release of Janice and Brenda? The—" Suddenly Bolan stopped short. "I don't believe this, Hal. You've already got Bolan out of Boston. A gesture of good faith?" The warrior raised an eyebrow. "Am I under arrest, Hal?"

"Hell, no," Brognola said curtly. "The President is asking you to be reasonable. You can't handle this one alone. Look, they took out your two friends and almost took out you, too, in twenty-four hours."

"Suppose you get a meeting with Cesare Frenchi," Bolan growled. He couldn't remember when he had been as angry. "What's the offer? What does he get for the return of his hostages?"

Brognola shook his head. "Nobody knows. Probably nothing. We don't know what he'll demand. The President wants a chance to work on it. I didn't have to tell you who killed Bonnie, and I didn't have to tell you the Vinnie connection. I trust you. I've never kept secrets from you."

"The President—"

Brognola interrupted. "I told the President I would give you the information. He didn't object and didn't ask me to keep anything from you."

"You're going to get in contact with Cesare," Bolan said quietly, "and you're going to negotiate. You're going to try to strike a deal. Of course, it will have to be a deal with some advantages for Cesare, or he won't agree."

"Well—"

"And when the word gets around, some other savage will kidnap the wife and child of some other federal officer and want to negotiate for some other advantage. Haven't we learned *anything* in the past twenty years?"

Brognola closed his eyes. "It's not my decision, Mack. The President listened to his advisers, and this was the decision they urged on him. The news media have the story now, and we can't do just what we want to do."

"What do you expect me to do?"

"I've got you a room in a motel in Arlington. It's safe, and guarded by a crack security team. Take forty-eight hours to rest. Then I'll come back and tell you what's going on. Maybe by then the President will want you to do it your way."

"Forty-eight hours," Bolan repeated grimly. "How much more will Cesare Frenchi maim Janice Elliott in forty-eight hours?"

BOLAN COULDN'T REMEMBER the exact words, but he recalled that some author once wrote something to the effect that nothing clears a man's mind like the certainty he will be hanged in the morning. Whether he had the quote right or not, a thought like that cleared *his* mind. The certainty that Janice and Brenda remained in the clutches of a crazed beast seized his mind and focused all his thought. Irrelevancies were pushed aside. He had one clear purpose, and it dominated.

Maybe that made it easier. It had been perfectly easy to walk out of the Arlington motel without the slightest interference by the guards Brognola had said were there to protect special guests like him. In fact, he didn't even go to his room; he walked out the back door of the motel and was in the parking lot looking for a cab before Brognola's car was out of sight.

A little later, from a telephone booth in downtown Washington, he placed a call to Boston. He was lucky; he caught Russ Caldwell at home. His stay at the Farm had been brief. Carla Caldwell had refused to remain—she had wanted to return home.

"How mad are you at the guy who broke Tom Dundee's arm and leg?" he asked.

"Damn mad."

"Mad enough to help me do something about it?"

"Do I get hurt? I hear friends of yours seem to have a way of—"

"I can't promise," Bolan interrupted. "What I need is an airplane ride to California. Right now."

"California?"

"It's important, Russ."

"Can you come up with some money? For the airplane, I mean."

"One way or another."

"Okay, you've just chartered a Lear. Be at Logan in half an hour."

"I'm in Washington."

"Washington? You don't make anything easy, do you? Okay, get yourself out to Dulles. I'll pick you up at the general-aviation terminal. Couple of hours or so."

Bolan slept on the flight, waking only when Caldwell landed at Albuquerque.

When they landed at Van Nuys he took half an hour to sit down to breakfast with Caldwell in the airport. By 9:00 a.m. he was in a rented car, on his way to hunt down Vinnie Frenchi.

CESARE FRENCHI STOOD at the front door of his old, white frame house on Block Island, staring thoughtfully at the Atlantic. The first time he had seen this house—when it had belonged to Grotteria—the front lawn had extended more than fifty yards to the edge of the bluff, where the land fell away to the ocean, fifty or sixty feet below. Now more than half that land was gone. They said a house like this had maybe another twenty years before it fell over and was taken by the sea. He shrugged. Twenty more years was enough.

Maybe it hadn't been such a good idea to snatch the two women. It had made heat. And, of course, now he could never let them go. The older broad couldn't complain about the way her finger had been taken—by a guy who knew what he was doing, using an anesthetic. Hell, he'd done it neatly. But she did complain, and if she got out of here she *would* complain, loud and long, for the reporters and cameramen, showing her stump. Talk about heat . . .

Sugar he could handle, the Commission he could handle, eventually, when he made them understand. Bolan— Well, how else could he have handled Bolan? And now the word was, somebody had done him two big favors: Lug Lugano and Bonnie, for Pete's sake! That ungrateful bitch had been working for Bolan, which explained a lot of things. Well, she'd been taught her lesson.

"Phone."

"Hmm?"

"Phone. It's your brother, Vinnie."

Cesare turned. "Okay, but don't ever walk up behind me like that again. You got it? Don't you ever."

He walked into the house, the spacious nineteenth-century house that had been the pride and joy of old Grotteria. The rooms were sparsely furnished, and no rugs or carpets hid the beauty of the marble floors. It had been a summer home, where Grotteria and his fat wife and kids had pretended to respectability.

The telephone was where it had always been, in the middle of the living room, near the windows that overlooked the shaded porch and afforded a view of the ocean. It was the only telephone in the house. Grotteria had tried to call for help on that telephone when he realized the Frenchi Family had come to take him out. If he'd had a phone in his bedroom, who knows what might have happened?

"Yeah?"

"Cesare? Vinnie."

"Twenty years and no talk. Now I can't get rid of you. What is it now, Vincenza? More orders from the Commission?"

"Nothing from the Commission," Vinnie replied. "Something from me. Listen, Cesare. For once in our lives—though you don't seem to see it that way yet—we're working together on something. And we got a loose end, Cesare. If the Family's going to be together on something, let's make it *all* the Family."

"Whose Family? Don Gaspare's—or Don Cesare's?"

"You're not a don, Brother."

"I'm as much a don as the cheap old Sicilian you work for," Cesare said with cold anger.

"Well, never mind that. Listen to me. The word now is that somebody high in the federal government is going to try to get in touch with you. He'll want to talk about the terms on which you'll release the two women you're holding. He—"

"Ha! You and the Commission told me it was a mistake to—"

"Cesare," Vinnie said firmly, "be damned careful. You can't get much for the Elliott women. Believe me, you can't. But you can get something we both have to want."

"What's that, Vincenza?" Cesare asked scornfully.

"Nina. Get them to let her out, let her go to Sicily."

He was talking about their sister, the one who was serving a life term in Framingham, the penitentiary for women.

"Are you out of your mind?" Cesare laughed. "I wouldn't pay a nickel to get Nina out of Framingham. Hell, I could have done it before now. What'd Nina ever do for Cesare, huh? What did Nina ever do for me? Anyway, she lives better in the ladies' slammer than she'd live in Sicily. I don't think she'd be grateful to us for getting her out of stir so she can go live in a pigpen."

"Cesare..."

"Forget it. Now tell me about this Sugar who's going to call. How's he going to know where to find me?"

"He isn't. The question is, can I tell them where to contact you?"

"No! Let them talk through *you*, Vincenza. They want to make a deal? Make a deal for me, *consigliere*. You report it to me. Then we'll see."

"Suppose I make a deal that includes Nina?"

Cesare laughed into the telephone.

VINNIE FRENCHI MIXED himself a Bloody Mary and carried it with him as he left the house and walked down to the beach. At noon his wife was still in bed—gorgeous, stupid thing, twenty years younger than he was, entertainment but no companion in life, certainly no partner. She'd hung one on last night, in celebration of his return from New York. In fact, she'd hung one on so bad that he'd slept with one of her friends—slept with her without ever learning her name—and had been hugely amused this morning when the girl begged him to make sure his wife, her friend, never found out.

Sure. Would she care?

This kind of thing, what some people called the California life, had long since ceased to mean much to Vinnie Frenchi. He lived well, ate well, drank well, made love when he wanted and generally with whatever girl he wanted. He worked for a man who demanded absolute obedience and loyalty, and otherwise was easy to get along with, and didn't fight the world the way Cesare had always thought necessary.

He was respected the way Cesare would never be. Look at the way the Commission had taken his advice about the Bolan-and-Boston business. He had no blood on his hands, not directly anyway. If the Sugars ever got him . . . Five years was the worst they could do to him.

Pup was his friend. That was what he called his Maltese dog. Pup was a smart little white fellow, ever his friend, ever lively. The dog cavorted ahead of him as Vinnie walked down to the sand, wrapped in a big white towel and carrying his Bloody Mary.

His house was on a cove, and he owned all the beach front, so much beach that he didn't have to wear swim clothes. He dropped the towel and spread it out on the soft, dry sand. He gulped down most of the Bloody Mary, then pressed the glass into the sand. Next to the glass he placed the small revolver he always carried to the isolated beach. Vinnie stretched out, nude, in the sun.

SOUTHERN-CALIFORNIA CASUAL. Bolan knew it well. He'd rented a white Dodge convertible and drove along the coast road, looking for Vinnie Frenchi's house.

He drove past number 448, taking a good look as he went by. The house was below the road, white stucco with a red tile roof. Very California. The grounds were immaculately groomed and trailed down to the edge of the Pacific. A very nice style of life for anyone. For a killer.

The warrior drove on for a half mile, then turned and came back to where he could stop and pull the white Dodge to the side of the road and leave it without its being conspicuous—on this road, a new white Dodge convertible wasn't noticeable.

Making himself inconspicuous, Bolan walked along the road barefoot, wearing only his white tennis shorts and carrying the Beretta under his towel. An unthreatening sun lover.

He walked down the broad driveway of 448, strode boldly to the door and touched the doorbell button.

"Yeah?"

The belligerent face of a Mafia soldier peered through the slightly opened door.

"I came to see Vinnie. Cesare sent me."

The hardman tried to shove the door shut, saying "No Vinnie here, never heard of no Cesare," but Bolan pushed the door against him, forcing the hardman back.

"I don't think you understood me, guy," he growled. "Vinnie's brother sent me."

And then it was as Bolan had anticipated. The hardman went for his pistol, and Bolan was forced to drop him.

The silenced Beretta made only an indistinct pop, and the guy stumbled back and fell, still grabbing awkwardly for his pistol as his heart ceased to pump blood.

Bolan stepped inside the house and quietly closed the door. He walked down the slate-paved center hall of the beach house, past the kitchen on the left, the dining room on the right, and into the oversized living room with its immense expanse of glass facing the Pacific.

No sound. Maybe Vinnie Frenchi was guarded by only one man.

He looked around. Evidently there had been a stormy party here last night. Maybe other hardmen were sleeping. He looked out at the beach to see a naked man stretched out on a big white towel. A little white dog scampered around him, chasing the breakers and barking.

Vinnie, most likely.

There was a long history between Bolan and Vinnie Frenchi, as there was between Bolan and Cesare. If either one of them had contented himself with hating Bolan and doing everything he could to destroy Bolan, well, that he could understand. War was war, after all—and this was war—and war had its rules. But these two made no pretense of adhering to any kind of rules.

He gripped the Beretta in his right hand, recovered it with the white terry-cloth towel and stepped out on the deck.

Silence. If there were other hardmen in the house, they didn't stir. The naked man on the towel looked to be asleep. The little white dog looked up, momentarily interested in the man who had come out onto the deck, but two gulls ventured into what he considered his territory, and he chased after them.

Bolan walked down toward the man on the towel. After a moment, he reached him.

"Private beach, fellow," Vinnie Frenchi murmured, not yet alarmed.

"Hi, Vinnie."

Vinnie Frenchi opened his eyes and looked up at the man who sat beside him on the sand. "Oh, Jesus Christ."

Bolan shook his head. "Not even close."

"Bolan..."

Vinnie Frenchi sat up and looked around, checking to see whether Bolan was alone. He made no effort to conceal his nudity.

"One of your bodyguards did his job," Bolan said. "If there are others...scream."

Frenchi glanced at the white towel that obviously concealed a pistol. "Hell..." he breathed. "Bolan. I don't know much about you, but I have to figure every man can be reasonable."

Bolan nodded. "Every man can be reasonable," he agreed.

"So... Between you and me. I mean, Bolan, in the long run, you can kill me, you can kill my brother, you can kill a hundred other guys like us—and, in the long run, what good will it do you? You kill me, which you can do in the next ten seconds, and another guy pops up in my place. So...?"

"Maybe. On the other hand, I can take the position that whatever I can do to get rid of people like you is a benefit to humanity."

"Shit, sure," Vinnie agreed nervously. "And who comes next? You think nobody steps into my shoes? You whack me out right now, Don Gaspare this afternoon, Cesare tomorrow, and God-knows-who next week, and do you think our kind will disappear? Come on, Bolan. Live! You can't reform the world. Better men than you have tried, over the centuries."

"You're trying to tell me what they did meant nothing?" Bolan asked.

"That the blood of martyrs meant nothing? I'd like to tell you that the blood of live men means something. Mine, my God. And yours, too. The government is opening negotiations—"

"With animals."

Vinnie Frenchi nodded. "I left Boston because I was afraid of my brother. I'm not like him."

"Yes, you are," Bolan said coldly.

Vinnie Frenchi frowned. "Meaning . . . ?"

"You sent Tally Minozzo to kill me. He tried."

"He killed Bonnie Hennings, but he wasn't ordered to."

"No. Of course not."

Frenchi turned his face toward the ocean and stared at the distant horizon. "You and I can make a deal, Bolan."

"I doubt it."

"You better listen. I know where the two Elliott women are. We can even things up between you and me. I'll tell you where Cesare is, and the women, and you forget whatever it was you came here for, because you got something better."

Bolan, too, stared out to sea. "I'm listening."

"Is it a deal? I tell you where Cesare and the Elliott women are, and you drop the idea of killing me."

Bolan nodded. "It's a deal."

"Okay. My brother knocked over the old don who once ran the Boston territory he has now. Cesare took everything that was Grotteria's. Everything—his rackets, his young wife, who he played with for a while, then dropped. Everything, including a big old house on Block Island, where the old man used to go for summer vacations. That's where he is now. That's where the women are. I talked to him an hour ago. He's there."

"Where on the island is this house?"

Vinnie shrugged. "I've never been there, but where could it be? Block Island's not so big. Anyway, that's where he is. On Block Island. You want proof? We can go into the house, and I'll call him. You can listen on an extension. I'll ask him how's things on Block Island."

"I believe you."

Vinnie continued to stare at the Pacific. "You wonder why I'm so quick to tell you. I'll tell you something else. The Commission has a contract out on Cesare. They want him dead as much as you do. And as for me... As for me, I don't care."

"Brotherly love."

Vinnie sniffed. "Yeah. Love ..." Then he made the fatal mistake of lunging for an object half-buried in the sand.

Bolan had to move the muzzle on the Beretta only a few degrees to point it directly at Vinnie Frenchi's armpit. The silenced pistol coughed and drove a 3-round burst of 9 mm slugs through Frenchi's ribs, through his lungs, grazing his heart. Vinnie Frenchi had tried to make his last deal.

HALF AN HOUR LATER a motor launch entered the cove and approached the beach. The driver, alone in the boat, was a tall black woman in a tiny iridescent-blue bikini. She guided the boat with practiced skill, bringing it as close to shore as she dared without risking its being carried onto the beach by the breakers. She cut the motor and threw out an anchor. After testing the depth with an oar, she dived smoothly off the stern and swam to the sand.

Guiseppe Rossi had called Salina Beaudreau. He'd said Bolan was on his way to California, and that if she could be there herself in the morning, she would be with Vinnie Frenchi when Bolan came to try to knock him off.

She'd flown in a private jet, furnished by the Rossi Family, and had been met at the airport by one of Don Gaspare's wise guys, who had driven her to the marina. He had planned to come with her, but she'd told him very firmly that she worked alone. So he'd told her how to recognize the Frenchi house when she saw it from the water. He'd told her the name of Vinnie's bodyguard and that Vinnie was at home, probably sleeping on the beach.

And there he was, sleeping on the beach stark naked.

"Vinnie . . . Vinnie!"

Damn! Maybe she had underestimated Mack Bolan. Maybe he was as good as his reputation.

She looked around. Nothing moved in the house. Probably Bolan had whacked the bodyguard, too. And maybe he was still in there. She hadn't carried a gun with her on her swim to the beach. This was no time to encounter Mack Bolan.

Salina Beaudreau frowned for a moment at the body of Vinnie Frenchi. All the blood was under him, soaking the sand. A dozen people could have walked past him since he died, and none of them would have realized he'd been hit. Except for three shell casings lying near him.

Well, let the cops figure it out. They'd have a job. The tide was coming in fast, and in another quarter hour, the body would be washed out to sea, together with those shell casings.

Salina walked into the surf and swam toward the launch. She smiled to herself at the thought of the reaction she was going to get when she told Don Gaspare's wise guy that the Nicolosi *consigliere* was dead. That was going to be almost as funny as the reaction she'd get from Rossi when she told him how fast Bolan had moved.

15

While Russ Caldwell was flying Bolan to Los Angeles, his wife and son waited at home. Avid Red Sox fans, they watched that night's game on television, then became interested in a movie on cable. A man sat in a car on the street outside their house, trying to stay awake as he kept watch on their property.

The Caldwells lived in a modest suburban neighborhood. Their house was twenty-five feet from the street, and there was no paved walk from the street to their door—visitors had to walk up the driveway. The front lawn was planted with two beds of flowers, each surrounded by low shrubbery; a blue spruce grew beside the driveway, and a maple toward the edge of the lot. The Caldwell's green Ford was parked on the asphalt driveway.

For three hours the watcher had focused his attention on the Caldwell home, and he'd seen nothing out of the ordinary.

A pair of teenagers had parked in the shadows on the opposite side of the street, confident that no one was about at midnight to see what they did. But the watcher had been sitting there in the dark for so long, that his pupils were wide open, and he did see. He didn't care, but he did see. It took them about ten minutes, and afterward the boy walked the girl to the door, kissed her chastely and saw her enter the house and kiss her mother on the cheek.

Traffic stopped about midnight. People who had been out came home and went to bed. The street grew darker and quieter.

Still, there were lights in the Caldwell house and the watcher guessed they were watching television.

And then, about a quarter to one, a Mercedes drove slowly along the street. It cruised past the Caldwell house, turned right at the end of the block and disappeared, then appeared again and did a second drive-by.

The watcher slipped out of his car and trotted up the Caldwell's front lawn, found a shadowed place not far from the front door and settled to wait.

The Mercedes cruised past again, this time stopping for a moment to let a man out. The vehicle sped away as the man strode up the Caldwell driveway.

The waiting man reached inside his jacket and withdrew a Bali-Song—a special, deadly knife he'd been introduced to during his Navy service in the Philippines. The six-inch blade was hidden inside its folding double-handles, and the watcher deftly rotated the handles to expose the razor-sharp stainless-steel blade, as sharp as a razor.

The man from the Mercedes reached the small porch. He stood at the door, but he didn't reach for the doorbell button. Instead he checked the knob to see whether the door was locked, which it was. It didn't matter. He had a set of small tools, and quickly, efficiently set to work to pick the lock.

Technically, the watcher needed more evidence than that. Technically. But sometimes "technically" didn't work. He sprang out of the shadows and drove the blade of the Bali-Song into the man's back, pulled it out and drove it in again. The man staggered back until a third blow sliced across his throat.

If the watcher was wrong, it was simple murder. In fact, it was murder anyway, contrary to every rule. He cleaned and refolded the Bali-Song and returned it to the leather sheath under his jacket, where it rested against the holster of his .38 revolver. He dragged the body—it wasn't a body, as a few weak breaths still bubbled through the knife wounds—into the shadows.

He took surgical gloves from his pocket, donned them and searched the dying man. Okay. He hadn't been wrong. He had committed murder, but it had been the murder of a hit man. A hit man carrying a silenced 9 mm Glock-17 automatic—an ugly but rugged pistol.

He knelt in the shadows and waited again. The driver of the Mercedes would surely return.

The car kept circling the block, but finally came to a stop. The driver switched out the lights and strode into the Caldwell driveway. She was a short, chubby, dark-haired woman, carrying an Uzi, which was capable of spraying a continuous stream of 9 mm death.

Conspicuously impatient, she took the two steps onto the Caldwell porch and grabbed the doorknob. When she couldn't open the door she stepped back and raised the muzzle of the Uzi, intending to gain entry fast.

The watcher took aim with the Glock and shot her in the chest. She stumbled down the steps and fell on the lawn. A second shot into her face made sure she stayed down.

He took five minutes to drag the two bodies to the Mercedes and lift them into the trunk, then tossed the Glock and Uzi in on top of them. He went back and used the Caldwell's garden hose to quietly wash the blood off the porch and grass. They needn't ever know that two hitters had come for them tonight.

He locked his car, deciding to return for it before dawn, and drove away in the Mercedes. He'd park it somewhere.

Sooner or later the two contract killers would be found, and there would be a mystery. For everybody.

This wasn't the way it was supposed to be done. He'd violated his oath. He'd violated— Yeah, sure. And he'd saved the lives of Caldwell's wife and son.

As he drove off, Special Agent Robert DiRosario shrugged off thoughts of his oath and began to think about where he'd abandon the Mercedes and the two corpses.

"DAMMIT, YES, he's human!" Cesare Frenchi yelled into the telephone. "He was flyin' around in a damn private jet. That's how he did it."

Cesare had received word of his brother's death in mid-evening, indirectly from Salina Beaudreau, through Joe Rossi, who then phoned DeMaioribus in Providence, the only member of the Commission who knew where to call him. Now DeMaioribus was on the telephone again, telling him two contract hitters had been found dead in the trunk of a leased Mercedes. Did Cesare know what they'd been doing?

Sure he knew what they'd been doing, though he didn't admit anything to DeMaioribus. They'd been sent to make a damned airplane jockey know what a big mistake he'd made.

DeMaioribus wondered how Bolan could have killed Vinnie in L.A. in the morning—midafternoon, Boston time—and still been back in Boston in time to take out two hitters sometime in the night. Was the guy human?

"Your hitters, Cesare?" DeMaioribus asked.

"Sometimes."

"This time?"

"Could be."

"Another civilian? Another Sugar?"

Cesare considered before he answered. DeMaioribus was not a man to trifle with. "Not a Sugar," he said. "A civilian. I've got to protect—"

"So Bolan takes out your hitters. How'd he even know? They get the civilian?"

"I don't know yet. I don't think so."

"This civilian. Would it have made heat?"

Cesare pondered that quickly. He didn't know, he hadn't even thought about that, much. He couldn't let an airplane jockey defy him. That was what he'd been thinking about.

"We got enough heat, Cesare," DeMaioribus intoned solemnly.

Cesare knew the man's voice, knew he meant business. "Maybe so."

"No maybe. For sure. It's enough, Cesare. You gotta cool it."

Cesare Frenchi drew a deep breath and recovered his defiant courage. "Yeah? Well, I tell you what, Lucky. The Feds want to talk to me. *Talk*. They want to offer a price for the two women I have. How about that?"

"Is Bolan coming to these talks?"

"I'm going to ask for Bolan's balls on a silver platter."

"I got words for you, Cesare," DeMaioribus replied. "You keep those two women alive. You kill them, the heat's comin' down on every Family. Heat like we never saw before. And whoever that civilian is, you leave him alone, Cesare. You lay low. You don't, you're declaring war on every other Family in the United States."

Cesare's chin dropped and his mouth fell open. This was a real threat.

"We'll put a ten-million-dollar contract on you, Cesare. Ten million. The biggest ever. Bigger than the one on Bolan."

"Jeez, Lucky..."

"We're gonna get Bolan. We're workin' on it. Twice we've almost got him in the past few days. We figured he was goin' after Vinnie, and we had the best hitter in the business out there to catch Bolan when he went after Vinnie. But because of that jet you say he flew, Bolan got there first, even though our hitter was sent to Los Angeles in *our* private jet."

"My hitters were after the wife and son of the pilot," Cesare said weakly.

"That's dumb, Cesare. Now you listen to me. Sooner or later, Bolan's gonna find out where you are. And when he does, he'll come after you. That makes you the bait in our trap."

"Bait?"

"That's what you are now, Cesare. Bait. You and the two Elliott women. So you sit still. No more adventures. You keep those women alive, and you stay where you are. A lotta guys are comin' to Block Island. We're gonna be ready for Bolan."

BOLAN ASKED CALDWELL to fly over Block Island during the return trip to Boston. Caldwell asked Air Traffic Control to cancel his flight plan, then he swung the Lear out over Long Island Sound and headed east toward the island.

About fifteen miles east of Montauk Point, the easternmost point of Long Island, and ten miles south of Judith Point, the southernmost point of Rhode Island, Block Island was also about forty miles south of Providence and was part of the state of Rhode Island. Irregular in shape, it was only five miles from north to south and less than three miles wide. It was home to a small year-round population and a summer resort for a considerably larger crowd of seasonal tourists, who came to enjoy its isolation and the beautiful, surf-battered beaches of the south shore. Though there were cars on the island, the most popular form of transportation was bicycles and mopeds. There were no big hotels, only small, white frame inns. Tourists came on a ferry that ran back and forth from Point Judith. A smaller number came in aircraft that landed on the single runway of the island airport.

"Can you put this plane down on that runway?" Bolan asked Caldwell.

Caldwell shrugged. "Could..." he said.

"But the whole island would know it."

"I don't know what you did in California," Caldwell said. "I don't think I want to know. But our landing at Van Nuys didn't mean much to anybody. If we put this bird down on that runway... It'd be a feat of piloting to start with, and everybody on the island would be talking about it."

"If I was looking for a house on the south shore...?"

"Above the cliffs. See the breakers below? That's the open Atlantic beating on the island, slowly washing it away. The lighthouse there will be in the ocean before too long. The houses, the same."

Bolan used binoculars to study the layout of the island. All the houses on the south bluff faced the Atlantic. They were big, old houses, and there weren't many. A single road ran from the airport to these homes and then wound to the east and down into the town.

"Can you land there at night?"

"Sure."

"Tomorrow night?"

"I know you're doing something good, and I wish I could say yes and let it go at that. But I have to ask about money. These airplanes don't belong to me."

"I'll take care of that."

WHEN CALDWELL TAXIED the Lear to the Dundee ramp in the last light of day, Hal Brognola was waiting. Bolan could see him on the tarmac, striding back and forth, chewing on a big cigar. He'd had to anticipate that the big Fed would be as mad as hell.

"I don't need to tell you what the President said," Brognola said gruffly.

"You work for the President. I don't."

Brognola looked away from Bolan, at a Lufthansa 747 settling down on the runway. From this ramp you were much closer to the runways than you ever were in the passenger terminal; you had a far more intimate look at the big birds coming in.

"You and I can't be on opposite sides of things, Striker."

"We aren't. You know I'm right. The difference is, you're willing to take orders, and I'm not."

Caldwell stepped down from the Lear. He eyed Bolan and the portly, grim man, so obviously a federal agent. Caldwell walked into the hangar.

Brognola blew a long, noisy sigh that fluttered his lips. "I'm going to tell you something," he said. "If you ever quote me—even quote me back to myself—I'll deny it. I'm supposed to tell you the President is so disillusioned with you that you're close to being persona non grata again. That's what he said in the presence of the attorney general and the director of the CIA. Afterward, to me alone, he said he admired your damned courage."

Bolan began to walk toward the hangar, but Brognola touched his arm and pointed to his car.

"Let's go have something to eat," the big Fed suggested. "I've got some things to tell you."

IT WAS THE FIRST real food he'd had during the past twenty-four hours. Bolan and Brognola sat in a rear booth of a dimly lit steak house, away from prying eyes and indiscreet ears.

"What makes the attorney general mad is that Cesare Frenchi broke off our talks. No word as to why, but it has to be because you killed Vinnie."

"Vinnie killed Bonnie," Bolan said quietly.

Brognola nodded. "I knew you'd consider that reason enough. Did you let emotion get in your way?"

"I'm entitled to emotions, just like anyone else. But if you want to know the truth, I took out Vinnie so Cesare would break off the talks."

"I'm not sure the President's not relieved," Brognola replied. "Don't quote me on that, either. Okay. So the negotiations have stopped."

"They had to stop."

"I won't argue that. We've covered the subject. But I'm getting intel from all around the country. All the Families are sending in their hitters. You aren't going to be facing just the Frenchi crowd, or what's left of it... Striker—"

"Do you know where?" Bolan asked bluntly.

Brognola shook his head. "Do you?"

Bolan had decided not to tell him. "Not yet. Not for sure. But I will know before long. What I want to know is, will you supply the hardware?"

"You can't go in by yourself."

"It's the best way," Bolan said. "The only way. But I need what a man needs. Okay? Yes or no?"

"If I say no, you'll go without," said Brognola.

"I've done it before."

"It's that important?"

"What we do is important, Hal. I don't have to lecture you on that. This time... The Frenchis? No. I suppose not.

The two Elliott women? Maybe. But the whole deal. The big deal. We can't step back. That's why I screwed up the negotiations, and that's why I'm going after Cesare Frenchi—with your help or without it."

Brognola removed the wrapper from another big cigar. "Give me your laundry list."

"YOU...TOOK two of them out?"

Agent DiRosario raised his glass of Chianti and sipped appreciatively. "Unofficially. I can't tell anyone else. I knew you'd understand."

"Understand..." Bolan muttered.

"Someone at Dundee is a Judas," DiRosario told him.

Bolan sat in a small Italian restaurant, watching Robert DiRosario eat his dinner. He'd paid too little attention to the agent. The man was powerful. His solemn face bore the marks of tough experience and bore also the mark of commitment.

"It's coming to an end," DiRosario said. "With those two hitters gone, Cesare Frenchi is running out of resources."

"Reinforcements are coming in."

"For you?"

Bolan shook his head. "I'm used to working alone. I've done it before. Many times. Most of the time, in fact."

"They've got a million-dollar contract out on you. And tough guys coming in to bail out Frenchi. You need help."

"Well..."

"Don't try to talk me out of it, Bolan."

Bolan shook his head firmly. "Forget it."

"No way, man. I've already broken out of the corral. You can't get rid of me."

"I work in a special way," said Bolan.

"I took out the man last night with a Bali-Song. I can handle that kind of stuff. I didn't come to the FBI from law school or accounting school. I have experience in the hard games."

"I heard the Bureau was recruiting men with that kind of experience."

"I'm one of them. I came to the Bureau from the Navy. Counterinsurgency. Counterintelligence. I can back you up, big fellow. And you're going to need—"

"You can ruin your career."

"What's it worth if I back away from a deal like this?"

"I ought to say no to you."

"That's what you ought to say. Sure. Well, forget it. Deal me in, Bolan. That last finger was real, cut off the hand of Janice Elliott, and I'm coming with you to get the guys who're responsible. Anyway, you need me. You can play hero just so far."

Bolan nodded. "Okay, you're in."

16

Janice Elliott ate with her left hand. Her right hand was wrapped in a huge white bandage. From time to time Brenda offered to help with her meal, but Janice quietly shrugged her off and continued to pick listlessly at the platter of food that had been put before them. Three times a day one of the men brought in one big platter and cans of Coke for the two of them. No utensils. They had to eat with their fingers—even spaghetti. In other circumstances it might have been funny.

They were still chained ankle to ankle. Brenda had become listless and sat hour after hour staring at the walls. She had lost hope and spirit as she watched her mother's finger being crudely amputated. Though she hadn't said so, Janice understood that Brenda believed they were going to die, that there was no hope for them. For herself, Janice did believe there was hope. She didn't talk about it, for what point was there in speculating on what might happen?

The days passed slowly, and the women weren't sure how long they had sat in the underground room. But they could hear activity upstairs, and voices—harsh, argumentative voices. And one man who shouted in shrill, nearly hysterical tones.

Something was about to change.

"WE'RE TALKIN' about one man, dammit!"

"That one man, in the past forty-eight hours, has killed Tally Minozzo, my brother Vinnie, plus Vinnie's bodyguard, and a pair of hitters I sent to do a job in Boston," Cesare Frenchi raged. "You tell me how easy it's going to be to handle *one man*, punk."

"Actually," Salina Beaudreau interjected calmly, "it wasn't Bolan who killed your two hitters. Bolan was at least a thousand miles from Boston when that happened. A stone killer, cold as a stone, took out your man with a knife, then used your man's gun to take out the woman—but not until he'd put on rubber gloves so he wouldn't leave prints on the pistol. A cool workman, but no Bolan."

Cesare scowled at Salina. He wasn't used to being contradicted by a woman, but she was right. "Yeah..." he said.

She glanced around the room at the dozen mafiosi assembled in Frenchi's living room. "I suppose all of you have noticed that this is an island," she said sarcastically. "That means there are only two ways of getting here—by boat or by plane. You have guys watching the airport, Cesare?"

"Yeah."

"And the ferry dock?"

"Yeah, yeah." he snapped impatiently. What was she doing, taking over? "Yeah, I got all that taken care of."

"Well, you needn't have bothered. Call your guys back. No need to waste manpower. Bolan won't come by plane or on the ferry. Too obvious."

"So how else is he gonna come?" One of the wise guys asked. "You said—"

"Small boat, I imagine. Somewhere around the island. You don't have enough men to watch the whole perimeter of the island, so you concentrate your forces here. There's one place we *know* he has to come. Here.''

The wise guys exchanged glances, then looked inquiringly at their boss. Was he letting this woman take command? It could happen. Some of them knew her reputation. She'd spoken of a stone killer. *She* was a stone killer—a cold, efficient hitter, so damned good at what she did that she got only the best contracts, never failed, never got heat and collected the top fees in the business. The guys who knew who she was looked at her with a certain awe.

But some guys didn't know who she was.

''Who's the woman?'' asked a Cleveland thug called Paulie Parma. He cocked his hips and faced her with a sneer. ''Anything I can't stand, it's a mouthy broad.''

Salina stepped slowly toward him. Where the Baby Browning had come from, Paulie couldn't guess, nor could any of the other men who suddenly realized the weapon filled her hand. She was wearing a tight black suit of some elastic material that shaped itself to her body like a coat of paint. But wherever it had come from, she had the tiny .25 automatic in her hand, and it was pointed hard at Paulie's face.

''Hey, hey!'' he said, grinning and taking a step backward.

She extended her arm and pressed the pistol to the side of his head and pulled the trigger. The .25-caliber slug tore off his ear. One of the wise guys reached under his jacket to pull a pistol, but the muzzle of the Browning was instantly leveled at his face. He dropped the pistol back in its holster and turned up the palms of his hands.

The men watched Salina put the tiny automatic back into its holster—a sort of slit, opened into a little pouch just under her breasts. She sat down and lit a cigarette.

Someone went to the kitchen and came back with a towel for Paulie Parma to press to his head.

"I WAS A NAVAL OFFICER, dammit!" DiRosario protested.

"Well, it's a useful thing to know how to do."

"Takes practice," DiRosario grumbled.

"You're going to get practice. One jump, maybe two. We're going to do it the simplest way. Low pass, not far to fall."

"In the *dark*!"

"Moonlight," Bolan replied. "Anyway, we'll be wearing Gunderson goggles. It'll look as bright as day."

DiRosario glanced at Russ Caldwell, who was checking the oil level in one of the engines on the old twin-engined Beechcraft from which they would make their jumps. It was an ungainly-looking bird, with big radial engines, but Caldwell assured him and Bolan that it was an ideal aircraft for parachute jumping. At DiRosario's suggestion, which he had not fully explained even to Bolan, Caldwell had flown alone from Boston to Worcester, and they had driven there to meet him. He had suggested also that Caldwell file a flight plan saying he was flying to Pittsburgh, which he could amend by radio from the air, so that whoever was watching him wouldn't call Cesare Frenchi and report that Bolan and another man had taken off in a twin Beech, destination unknown but suspected.

DiRosario was concerned about Caldwell's family. He had stopped two hitters, but he couldn't be sure others wouldn't be sent. He had assigned two agents to watch the Caldwell house until Cesare Frenchi was destroyed, which would probably happen tonight.

They did their practice jumps into a field just west of the Connecticut River, near the town of Greenfield. Caldwell had many friends in the aviation fraternity, and a pair of young aircraft mechanics were happy to be paid to take the afternoon off to recover the two parachutists from the field and return them to the airport for another flight and another jump. DiRosario got in four jumps.

"Okay," Bolan said as the twin Beech lifted off after their last jump. "You ready for the big one?"

"Why not? I'm a certified idiot."

SALINA BEAUDREAU CRUSHED a cigarette and picked up a glass of wine.

"Let's get those two women on their feet," she said. "If we have to move them, we want them to be able to walk at least, if not to run. Make them jog around the room down there. Take the chain off. Get them moving, Cesare."

She hadn't given Cesare the courtesy of letting him hear her orders quietly. He continued to pretend that he did what she said in compliance with suggestions, not orders, and he resolved secretly that he would take care of her once this night was over—but in the meanwhile he did what she said.

"Maybe he won't come tonight," one of the wise guys suggested.

They had treated her with grudging respect since she shot the ear off Paulie Parma. They, too, were resolved to be rid of her sometime before morning. But in the meantime a smart, experienced hitter like this woman might be useful.

"Maybe he won't," she agreed. "So we all go to bed and don't worry about it."

"Yeah," said Cesare. "Yeah, sure."

"Bolan may not come tonight," she said. "Or tomorrow night. That'd be a joke—all this muscle lined up to meet him, and he doesn't bother."

"We're ready," one of the wise guys growled. "Crushers and biscuits." He meant killers with guns. "Unless he comes with an army—"

"He'll come when you don't expect him," Salina interrupted. "In a way you don't expect. He can blast you—"

"And blast the two women downstairs?" Cesare asked. "We got *them*, don't forget. Bolan's got to be careful."

FROM THREE THOUSAND FEET, Block Island at midnight looked like a crushed rubber ball lying on the moonlit surface of the Atlantic. The alternating white and green flashes of the airport beacon drew attention to the parallel strings of tiny yellowish lights that bordered the single runway. The shore was marked by the lights of scores of boats, houses and inns along the waterfront. The center of the island was mostly dark.

"All right," Bolan said to Caldwell. "Five hundred feet. Throttled back quietly, then go around and come back over the house full bore. Distract them."

"Gotcha." Caldwell pulled back his throttles and started his descent.

DiRosario shook his head. "Why so low? Hell, I need a minute or two to get my guts together."

"We could drift apart," explained Bolan. "The equipment chute could drift away from us. Or we could be spotted from the ground, which we don't want, even if it's not by one of Frenchi's boys. This way, we're going to be on the ground in about half a minute, together, and—with any kind of luck—just where we want to be."

The two men were dressed in identical black combat suits, with black paratroopers' boots. Bolan's Desert Eagle was snugged against his hip, and several extra magazines filled pouches on his belt. DiRosario had been trained on the .45 Colt, and that was what he'd chosen for his side arm. Both men had grenades clipped to their military harness and sheathed knives strapped on their thighs. Night-vision goggles illuminated their surroundings.

In addition, a Heckler & Koch G-11 caseless assault rifle was slung across each man's chest. It was a weapon occasionally favored by Mack Bolan, though DiRosario had never seen it before. Its smooth casing wasn't the G-11's unique characteristic. The top feature of the G-11 was the caseless rounds it fired—that is, bullets set in solid blocks of propellant, not in brass cartridge cases. When the G-11 was fired, the bullet exploded from the muzzle, driven by the hot gas that was all that remained of the propellant. There was no case to be expelled, no need for mechanical action to clear the breech before the next round could be loaded and fired. The G-11 could fire two thousand rounds a minute, and it loosed a 3-round burst in one-tenth of a second. The 4.7 mm slugs did their job by velocity rather than by weight. These G-11s were fitted with magazines that held one hundred rounds.

Other weapons and more ammunition and grenades were contained in a parachute-equipped pack that would be shoved out of the airplane just before the men jumped.

The road from the airport to the bluff above the beaches ran beside a freshwater pond, which was just south of the airport. Bolan meant to jump into the grassy land just west of that pond. From there he and DiRosario had less than a mile to cover to reach Frenchi's house.

Caldwell took the airplane well out to sea off the east coast of the island to get set on course well before they reached the jump point. The airport runway was noted on the chart as being a hundred feet above sea level. Caldwell stabilized the twin Beech at seven hundred feet. As he approached the shoreline, he pulled back his throttles until the twin engines were just idling, making almost no noise at all. Then he got rid of his extra two hundred feet of altitude, establishing a quiet glide down to five hundred, the jump altitude Bolan wanted.

Bolan had opened the door five miles out and had shoved the equipment pack to the edge, just short of its being pulled out by the slipstream. The rip cord was attached to a nylon strap that was tied to a lug inside the airplane.

"When we go, we go," Bolan reminded DiRosario. "Pack, you, me—quick. That way we'll be together when we hit the ground."

DiRosario nodded.

The door between the cockpit and the passenger compartment was lashed open. Russ Caldwell turned and said, "About a minute. Little less."

Except for a few lights slipping by underneath, the ground wasn't visible. Then they passed over a house where an outdoor light shone on the driveway, and they could see how low they were. After that, a gray glow— probably the surface of the pond. Then—

"Go!" Caldwell yelled.

Bolan kicked out the equipment pack, gave DiRosario a clap on the shoulder, and the man jumped. Finally Bolan jumped.

The warrior pulled his rip cord, then looked down and around. He could see two chutes floating just below him. He extended his feet to meet the ground, and in a few seconds he hit with a wallop.

"You okay?" he called to DiRosario, who was gathering his billowing chute from where Bolan stood.

"Muddy," DiRosario replied.

The ground was in fact muddy, marshy. At first Bolan couldn't spot the equipment pack, but then he pulled down his Gundersons and activated them, which gave him a clear view not just of the equipment chute spread out on the ground, but also of DiRosario slapping the mud off his black suit and checking his G-11.

Bolan trotted to the pack and began to unstrap it. It contained an MM-1 Multiround Projectile Launcher and an assortment of projectiles. He'd told Brognola he'd need the lethal weapon because of the odds he and DiRosario would have to confront. As usual the big Fed had come up with the goods.

"Look what's coming," DiRosario said, pointing.

Bolan looked up. The twin Beech was returning. Caldwell had swung out over the ocean to the west, pushed in his throttles and was coming out of the night as Bolan had instructed—full bore. He'd dropped his parachutists from a dark airplane, but now he was showing landing lights and blinding strobes. The radial engines were making an ungodly roar as the aircraft passed over the Frenchi house no more than a hundred feet above its roof.

MOST OF THE HARDMEN were sitting in the living room, drinking, smoking and playing cards. Cesare Frenchi was in a darkened bedroom above, not sleeping but brooding, staring from the windows. Salina Beaudreau was in another bedroom, also in the dark, also watching. She was wary, certain that Bolan would come tonight, running over and over in her mind his options, trying to decide how *she* would assault this house if it was her problem.

Janice and Brenda Elliott remained in the cellar, chained together again after an evening of being cruelly toyed with. Two men had come down, unchained the women and forced them to jog around the room, laughing at their discomfort and at how quickly they worked up a sweat. Both of them had supposed the humiliating exhibition was a preliminary to rape, and they'd been surprised as well as relieved when the two men became bored, chained them up again and left.

Paulie Parma lay on a cot on a screened-in porch at the back of the house. The boys had taped a rude bandage to his head, but the shredded remains of his ear hurt. Cesare had promised he could go back to the mainland tomorrow and see a doctor, but he had a little plan first. He was going to kill the black hitter if it was the last thing he ever did.

Paulie was the first one out of the house, and running toward the road when the plane roared over the house. He figured it was dropping a bomb and when he heard no explosion, he figured the bomb it had dropped was a dud.

The wise guys poured out the front and back doors, some raising weapons and firing after the Beech as it roared past the lighthouse and swept out over the Atlantic. Fourteen of them circled the house, brandishing Uzis, short-barreled automatic shotguns, and even a couple of M-16s.

They were thugs, but they weren't small-timers. Every one was a made man, and had killed, most of them more than once. What was more, some had had combat training and experience, if not in Vietnam then in the peacetime Army or Marines. They didn't run around the house like a mob. They formed two rough skirmish lines, one in front of the house, one behind. They then began a slow advance, one line toward the bluff, one down the slope toward the road.

Cesare had thrown himself to the bedroom floor as the Beech roared overhead. Now he crawled to the window and looked down. He could see his men forming lines to guard the house. They were following the plan—not to stay inside the house where they could be pinned down, if not in fact taken out, by one man's heavy fire, but to scatter outside the house in the dark and make Bolan wonder where each man was.

Cesare hadn't exactly told them his role in the plan. He checked his Walther PPK and the two extra clips of 7.65 mm ammo. Then he left the bedroom and started for the basement.

Salina Beaudreau remained in her bedroom, scanning the shadowy landscape below the house. Bolan was out there now; she had no doubt of it. Sure. He had parachuted onto the island, close to the house. He was just beyond the light, combat equipped and ready to come in. In a minute he'd make his move, and it would be like nothing Cesare Frenchi or any of the hitters sent by the Commission could possibly expect.

She was ready. If nobody else was, she was. The woman had changed into working clothes, a pair of camouflage combat fatigues. Her Baby Browning was in a pocket, and her Browning Hi-Power was sheathed in a holster that hung from her web belt. The Browning was unique in that its clip held not the eight or nine rounds usual to 9 mm and big-bore automatics, but thirteen.

The Mafia gunners were doing the right thing—spreading out, establishing a line of defense—but Cesare was still in the house. She'd bet on it. And she knew where to find him.

17

Bolan crouched in the shallow drainage depression at the edge of the road. DiRosario was to his left, two or three yards away. The two men had watched the gunners bolt from the house, and now they watched them moving away from it carefully. One by one the hardmen dropped to the ground, some concealed, all of them difficult to see.

"I make seven or eight of them," DiRosario said. "Plus maybe as many more on the other side of the house."

"We'll make our move quick. I want it all over before any neighbors come wandering over to find out what's going on."

The MM-1 is a short, fat weapon, looking something like a grossly swollen revolver. Each of its twelve chambers is loaded with a 38 mm projectile—high-explosives, tear gas, smoke, or flare—which can be fired in rapid succession, to a range of well over a hundred yards. Bolan had planned his attack and had loaded the first chamber with an explosive round, the next six with smoke rounds, the remaining five with explosives.

Bolan adjusted the optical sight on the MM-1 and fired an HE round at the house. It struck just to the right of the back door, where it blew in the door and opened a gaping hole in the wall. Then he fired a smoke round, which arrowed through the hole and burst inside, immediately filling the kitchen with dense white smoke. The remaining five smoke rounds followed in rapid succession. Within a minute smoke was drifting out of upstairs windows, which had been shattered by the concussion of the explosion.

Next Bolan focused on a utility pole. The MM-1 barked and the round struck the pole at its base. The explosion shattered the pole, and it toppled, tearing down electric and telephone wires. The house and vicinity went dark.

With the aid of the Gundersons, Bolan and DiRosario could see perfectly. They moved away from the road and slowly advanced toward the house. The wise guys couldn't see them but began to set up a coordinated field of fire down the slope—everything from military rounds from the M-16s to storms of buckshot from the shotguns. Bolan and the FBI agent dropped to the ground and began to fire 3-round bursts from their G-11s.

The rapid-fire bursts from the caseless rifles were terrifying. The sound was like a violent rip in the air, and the little slugs burst through a man and blew parts of him away. Men who saw others hit were, for a moment, petrified with fear.

The gunners who had run to the front, or southside, of the house realized now that the attack was coming from the north. They began to work their way along the east and west sides of the building. Bolan checked the wind and found a light breeze coming from the west. He delivered a one-two punch of tear gas near the hardmen, and the heavy gas spread over the lawn and crept slowly on the still air. The wise guys dropped back and started a wider course toward the rear of the house.

A man with a shotgun spotted Bolan. He popped up and began to pump loads of buckshot. DiRosario cut him down with a spray of 4.7 mm hornets.

"Too slow, this," Bolan grunted. "If they had a plan, this was what they had in mind—to slow us down. We've got to move. Let's go!"

DiRosario was ready. He'd unclipped two grenades and clutched one in each hand. Bolan nodded and pointed to the left and right, indicating where he would throw his grenades, showing DiRosario where he should throw his.

Bolan lobbed a grenade as a signal to DiRosario. The FBI man tossed both of his, and Bolan threw his last.

The MU-50G grenades were loaded with steel beads packed in a smokeless, almost flashless explosive. The beads burst out of the explosions with deadly velocity, butchering anything within fifteen feet of detonation point. The spread was right, and the grenades felled five gunners. Bolan and DiRosario trotted past broken, writhing bodies.

They were past the rough line the Mafia soldiers had set up, and turned now and set their G-11s on autofire to mop up behind them. After two short bursts apiece, each man dropped to a crouch and trotted to the back of the house.

PAULIE PARMA HAD CRAWLED back to safety. To hell with this firefight. It wasn't his problem. He had a .45 in his belt, and he had a score to settle.

He hadn't noticed until he got to the side door, but the house was filled with choking white smoke.

Paulie glanced to the rear. All hell was breaking loose there—heavy firing, explosions. It was war. He crouch-walked to the front of the house and mounted the steps. Crossing the porch, he grabbed open the front door.

The smoke that rushed out was thick and tinged with a heavy chemical smell. And it was dark inside. There was no electricity. He plunged inside, thinking he could make his way to the basement door and go down where maybe the smoke hadn't penetrated—where he expected to find something interesting. But he couldn't go forward. Paulie Parma retreated to the porch.

THE SMOKE HADN'T penetrated to the basement. Cesare Frenchi could see where he was and what he was doing. He had a battery-powered lantern, which was standard equipment at the summer house—electrical failures on the island weren't infrequent. It afforded him plenty of light for what he had gone down there to do.

Cesare had cuffed the Elliott women's hands behind their backs, then had taken the chain off their ankles.

"We're leavin', honeys," he announced. "Don't worry about how. I know. I'm smarter than some people think."

He knew there was a root cellar adjacent to the basement and that you could go through a wooden door and enter a dark, damp, dusty chamber where past generations had stored potatoes and other root foods. There was an outside exit from the root cellar, through a wooden trapdoor in the front yard, about two or three yards from the foundation of the house. It was in the dark and sheltered by shrubs that had been planted around it to shield the porch from a view of a dilapidated old door. A man coming out of the basement that way was well beyond the heavy battle raging outside. Unknown to anyone else, he could reach the bluff and descend to the beach down a trail well-known to young people anxious to make their way down to a relatively secluded stretch of beach.

Let Bolan take the house. Let Bolan whack the men the Commission had sent and the Frenchi bodyguards. He, Cesare Frenchi, would take his important hostages and leave Bolan with his collection of corpses.

"On your feet, girls. We're makin' tracks."

The two women, trembling with fear, their faces red and swollen from crying and from the tainted air that they had been compelled to breathe, struggled to their feet.

The electric lantern shed a cold, glaring light on the wisps of smoke that hung in the air.

"H'lo, Cesare."

He spun around. Salina Beaudreau stood in the door.

"Good," he grunted. "I can use some help. You know—"

He stopped cold, seeing that her big Browning was leveled at him.

"Salina—"

"Cesare, you're a real sorry example of the human race."

"Don't kid around," he said curtly, mock-bravely.

"Sorry," she said, raising the muzzle of her Browning just a little.

"Hey! The guy you got a contract for is outside!"

"I'm lookin' at the guy I got a contract for," she replied, squeezing off a shot. The 9 mm slug cracked into Frenchi's ribs, crushing his left lung with steel and bone fragments. She fired a second time, the slug exploding his heart.

It was true that she had a contract for Bolan, but Salina was no fool.

"Ladies, we're moving out," she said. "I won't need you long, but for a little while you may be insurance for me. So move it. Ahead of me, up the stairs. When you get to the top, you'll be in smoke. Get a deep breath first, then when you get out run left. In three seconds you'll be out the front door, on the porch, where there's air. *Go!*"

Janice and Brenda were horrified. They'd never seen a man killed before, and they had just seen this tall black woman coolly murder Cesare Frenchi. They were afraid of her. The women trotted up the stairs into the smoke.

PAULIE PARMA WAS WAITING in the yard in front. The firing had died down, and it was likely that Bolan was inside, in the smoke. He could come out for air at any minute. If he walked through the front door, Paulie would earn a cool million dollars for the hit. If the black broad came out, he'd have her. Maybe he'd get them both. He knelt and aimed his .45 at the doorway.

And then a shape burst through the doorway, too fast. Nervous, he pulled the trigger and fired at the figure coming out of the smoke. It was one of the Elliott women, the mother! And he'd missed her.

The woman screamed, fell to her knees, then toppled on her face. The younger one followed quickly, shrieking.

Standing in the smoke, with heavy white wisps swirling around her like she was something straight from hell, was Salina Beaudreau. Her gun was up and pointing straight at Paulie.

He switched his aim to the left to get her in his sight, knowing it was too late. She was so cold... Her first slug tore into his belly. The pain was so intense that he wished for a second one. His wish was granted. The round ripped through the side of his head, through the wound she'd made when she shot his ear off. Pieces of his brain and skull flew against the trunk of a tree.

"You're not hurt," Salina said to Janice. "Get up."

Brenda tried to help her mother to her feet. But with her hands locked behind her, there wasn't much she could do. Janice managed to struggle painfully to her feet.

Salina had explored the house and the area carefully as soon as she'd arrived. She hadn't found the door to the root cellar, but she had found the narrow, twisting path down to the beach. Herding Janice and Brenda ahead of her, she moved toward the bluff and the opening to the path.

THE TWO MEN HADN'T brought gas masks, so it was difficult for Bolan and DiRosario to move through the smoke. Not so difficult as it had been for everyone else, though, since their Gunderson goggles gave them good vision even inside the choking dense cloud. They saw the windows, smashed them out, and gulped breaths of air as they moved through the house.

Bolan judged that they'd find the Elliott women in the basement. He found the door and led the way down.

"Cesare Frenchi," he said to DiRosario, pointing to the body lying on the floor in front of the fireplace.

"They've been here," DiRosario said. "The women. They've been kept here. Look at the mattresses, the food."

"Look at the chain."

"Somebody rescued them already, you think?" DiRosario asked, nodding toward the body of Frenchi.

Bolan shook his head. "They're somebody else's hostages now. They're just as valuable to somebody else as they were to Cesare."

DiRosario examined the body. "I'd guess he was shot within the last five minutes. The blood hasn't even begun to dry."

Bolan nodded and quickly led the way up the steps and out into the central hall of the house. They ran out onto the front porch.

"Look at that one." DiRosario pointed to the body of Paulie Parma. "We didn't kill him. What the hell's going on around here?"

"Nothing unusual when you're fighting mad dogs," Bolan replied. "They're sometimes just as interested in killing each other as in killing you."

"Where do you suppose the women are?"

Bolan glanced around. "Somewhere close. No cars have left here since we came."

The warrior sprinted across the front lawn, toward the edge of the bluff. He looked over, then unholstered the MM-1. He searched in his equipment bag until he found the flares, then loaded three chambers with flare rounds.

"Bob, back me. I'd guess the Mafiosi are all dead or in retreat, but there may be some left, looking to score on the big contract they've got on my head. Settle yourself behind those shrubs and be ready to take out anybody who comes around the house."

"Right."

"Be careful," Bolan cautioned. "The local police could be on their way."

Bolan carried the MM-1 to the lip of the bluff. The range of his night goggles didn't extend very far down the almost-vertical slope, so he took them off and let his eyes become accustomed to the faint, mist-inhibited moonlight. As he peered into the darkness below, he couldn't see anyone. He could, though, make out the boundary between rocks and sand, and he could see the ghostly white line of the surf.

He aimed the MM-1 toward the sand and fired a flare round. It flew silently through the air, hit the sand and burst into a white glare.

And there they were—Janice Elliott and her daughter, Brenda, bound in handcuffs, being herded along by a tall figure in combat fatigues. They were almost to the sand at the bottom of a trail.

Bolan stood stunned for a moment when he realized the figure was a woman—a black woman. She crouched and pointed a pistol upward, which was futile. Since the MM-1 launched its rounds by spring action, there had been no flash. She couldn't see where the flare had come from.

Bolan fired another flare, which landed on the sand a few yards from the first, and still she couldn't spot Bolan's location.

The black woman took shelter behind a big rock. The Elliotts ran away from her, east along the beach until they were almost out of the light cast by the flares. Bolan saw them stumble and fall, but he could see it was from exhaustion, not because the black woman had fired on them.

The woman came out from behind the rock and started to follow Janice and Brenda. Bolan took careful aim with the Desert Eagle. The big pistol roared and flashed, and a .44 Magnum slug blew a little crater in the sand just ahead of her. The woman retreated.

She'd seen where that shot came from and had heard the unmistakable authoritative flame and crack of a big handgun. She crouched behind her rock, out of sight.

Janice and Brenda had seen it, too. They scrambled to their feet and ran as best they could, hands fastened behind them, into the rocks beyond the circle of light.

The flares were going out. Bolan had one more chambered. He angled the MM-1 so that the projectile would land in front of the rock that sheltered his enemy. He still couldn't see her, but he knew she was there. He fired a .44 slug at the rock, to keep her respectful.

He heard the distinct crack of a 3-round burst from one of the H&K caseless rifles. DiRosario had fired on a hardman.

Bolan lowered the Gundersons over his eyes and scanned the lawn between the bluff and the house. The wise guy had dropped to the ground in a clump of bushes beyond the southwest corner of the house. DiRosario probably couldn't see him even with his night goggles. Bolan could—the man had a grenade and was looking for DiRosario.

The warrior rotated the wheel of the projectile launcher to put an HE round into firing position, took aim and loosed the round, which exploded at the guy's feet, blowing him into the air. The hardman had already pulled the pin on his grenade, and as his dead hand relaxed, its fuse was lit. The lethal orb exploded, blowing the already-dead hardman to bits.

"That was his grenade!" Bolan yelled at DiRosario. "Take 'em out fast!"

Bolan took more flares from the satchel and looked down over the bluff. The flares on the beach had burned out, leaving only sullen red chemical fires smoldering at three points on the wet sand. He loaded the MM-1 and fired two more.

Nothing. He couldn't see the black woman or the Elliott women.

Using the Gunderson goggles again, he sprinted down the winding trail among the rocks, toward the beach. It wasn't an easy trail, reversing and re-reversing, narrow, and at times requiring him to slip down a rock face. He wondered how Janice and Brenda had managed to do it with their hands cuffed behind their backs.

The warrior stood at the bottom of the path and waited for the flares to burn out. No point in giving his adversary the opportunity to take a shot at him. Then the Gundersons allowed him to explore the beach.

He found a pair of fatigues behind the rock where the black woman had sheltered, and a Browning Hi-Power. He looked out at the water. The evidence said that she had shed her clothes and swum out to sea. The mystery woman had gotten away.

As the warrior jogged along the sand, probing the shadows, he finally made out the shapes of two shuffling figures dead ahead. He called out to reassure them, then sprinted forward. Bolan couldn't help but think of the black woman and wonder about the part she had played in the Frenchi affair. No doubt she'd killed Lug and had the contract on the Executioner.

As the warrior drew Janice and Brenda Elliott into the protection of his arms, he had a feeling in his gut that he hadn't seen the last of that particular Mafia hitter.

Trouble erupts for Nile Barrabas and his men when an undersea Soviet war base pits them against their most deadly enemy.

THE BARRABAS WAR

JACK HILD

A full-scale war is about to break out when suspected acts of Turkish terrorism result in furious Greek retaliation. Barrabas and his elite mercenaries discover a state-of-the-art command station and a sinister Soviet plot lurking beneath the Aegean Sea!

The line between good and evil is a tightrope no man should walk. Unless that man is the Executioner.

BLOWOUT $3.95 ☐
Framed for murder and wanted by both sides of the law, Bolan escapes into the icy German underground to stalk a Mafia-protected drug baron.

TIGHTROPE $3.95 ☐
When top officials of international Intelligence agencies are murdered, Mack Bolan pits his skill against an alliance of renegade agents and uncovers a deadly scheme to murder the U.S. President.

MOVING TARGET $3.95 ☐
America's most powerful corporations are reaping huge profits by dealing in arms with anyone who can pay the price. Dogged by assassins, Mack Bolan becomes caught in a power struggle that might be his last.

FLESH & BLOOD $3.95 ☐
When Asian communities are victimized by predators among their own—thriving gangs of smugglers, extortionists and pimps—they turn to Mack Bolan for help.

Total Amount	$ _____
Plus 75¢ Postage	.75
Payment enclosed	$ _____

Please Print
Name: _____
Address: _____
City: _____
State/Prov: _____
Zip/Postal Code: _____

SMB-3

TAKE 'EM NOW

FOLDING SUNGLASSES
FROM GOLD EAGLE

Mean up your act with these tough, street-smart shades. Practical, too, because they fold 3 times into a handy, zip-up polyurethane pouch that fits neatly into your pocket. Rugged metal frame. Scratch-resistant acrylic lenses. Best of all, they can be yours for only $6.99.

MAIL YOUR ORDER TODAY.

Send your name, address, and zip code, along with a check or money order for just $6.99 + .75¢ for postage and handling (for a total of $7.74) payable to Gold Eagle Reader Service. (New York and Iowa residents please add applicable sales tax.)

Remove from pouch.

unfold once

unfold twice

and they're ready to wear

GES-1A

Gold Eagle Reader Service
901 Fuhrmann Blvd.
P.O. Box 1396
Buffalo, N.Y. 14240-1396

Offer not available in Canada.